GIOVANNI GUARESCHI

Duncan & Clotilda

AN EXTRAVAGANZA WITH A LONG DIGRESSION ❀ · ❀ · ❀

TRANSLATED BY L. K. CONRAD

FARRAR, STRAUS & GIROUX ❀ NEW YORK

DUNCAN & CLOTILDA

Giovanni Guareschi is the author of

THE LITTLE WORLD OF DON CAMILLO

COMRADE DON CAMILLO

MY HOME, SWEET HOME

A HUSBAND IN BOARDING SCHOOL

DUNCAN & CLOTILDA

DUNCAN & CLOTILDA

1

At 9 a.m. on May 14, 1905, the auxiliary schooner
Dolphin weighed anchor from the port of New Islip,
capital of a certain small country, and set out to sea.
Half an hour later, Mr. Duncan Fitzmorris heard a discreet knock at the door of his cabin, and this simple act
provoked a reasonable amount of pleasure in him, since
Duncan had in fact been waiting for that knock at his
door. To be more explicit, he was expecting the arrival
of Miss Clotilda Troll. Quite logical for him to expect
her, after the unique letter he'd received the night before:

My dear Sir,
Tomorrow my yacht will set out on a short cruise.
I'll expect you on board by 8:30 a.m. I'd like you to
be party to an interesting idea I've been mulling over
for quite some time now.
Thanks beforehand for coming. In the meantime,
please accept a little kiss from your
Clotilda Troll

Who had the face to turn down a kiss from Clotilda
Troll, the most beautiful, most famous, and richest girl
in New Islip? Only Duncan Fitzmorris—if he'd found
himself in normal circumstances—would have been in

a position to refuse her kiss. In fact, in different circumstances, he most certainly would have done so. But now, because of a single glass of castor oil, Duncan found himself in the most abnormal circumstances.

Duncan Fitzmorris was the scion of an extremely rich New Islip family and, more important, a man of character, something he'd inherited in equal parts from his father and his mother. From his father, Thomas Fitzmorris, he'd contracted the dislike for convention which caused the elder Fitzmorris to leave Duncan an orphan several months after he was born: Thomas was fed up with the extreme banality of drawing breath.

Considering the excessive dullness of life, Duncan hadn't had much fun. By the time he was nineteen and living with his uncle Philip, Duncan, despite the fact that he had all his uncle's money to spend, was thoroughly bored. But one day he came across a pastime which began to intrigue him: the profession of medicine. Duncan immersed himself in anatomy and biochemistry books for two years, at the end of which he crawled into bed groaning.

The three most famous surgeons in the city were called together, and to them Duncan described his symptoms so meticulously, located them so precisely, explained the irregularities provoked by the malady in his system so exactly that finally the three great surgeons looked at each other in triumph and intoned in chorus: "This is the most clear-cut, positively the most well-defined case of appendicitis in the annals of medical history!"

Then they assembled the medical student body in the university operating theater to demonstrate this most classic case of appendicitis.

The day of the operation arrived. The most famous of the three medical geniuses took up his scalpel, cut open Duncan's abdomen, and almost fainted with surprise. There, in front of his expert eyes, was the healthiest intestine he had ever observed. Not the shadow of appendicitis was apparent.

That time Duncan had enjoyed himself, but what hard work to manage those few entertaining moments! He'd had to study for an eternity to be able to describe an imaginary ailment with enough finesse to convince three prominent men of science. He'd also had to let himself be opened up, just to see the looks on the faces of the three most respected surgeons in the world.

Duncan really hadn't had many good times in his life. It might be said that he'd only truly enjoyed himself twice: the first time with this joke on the three surgeons; the second time when he put something over on the whole population of New Telford. At that point Duncan was twenty-five. He moved to New Telford under an assumed name and bought a large store downtown. He papered the avenues with posters, filled the newspapers with announcements, and of course the people ran to have a look. They were stunned.

Duncan's store didn't have a thing in it. Not so much as a tack in the walls, not a safety pin in the showcases. The signboard outside had one word printed in bold letters: N O T H I N G .

The people laughed at first, thinking it was a good joke; then they started to think it might be a publicity stunt. Then they began to get annoyed. Every morning Duncan, in deadly seriousness, would open out the shutters and the awnings and install himself on a stool —the only piece of furniture—in the center of the huge store. Not a word, not a gesture. The people were offended. "Nothing," they read out loud to each other, snorting in disapproval. Every once in a while one of them would close in for a better look.

"All right, why don't you tell us what you really sell here?" these onlookers invariably shouted at Duncan.

"Nothing," Duncan would reply with great dignity.

This went on for three months and every day the people grew more indignant. Finally one morning a ruddy-faced fat man walked into the store and planted himself menacingly in front of Duncan.

"Nothing?" he asked grimly.

"That's right, nothing," replied Duncan, nodding.

"For how much?" the ruddy man asked, still grim.

"From ten pounds and up."

"Give me some for thirty pounds," the man demanded, showing his teeth and pulling out his wallet.

Duncan pocketed the money and blew on the man's open hand.

"There you are," he said. "All right?"

"Fine, thank you." The ruddy man sighed, as if a huge weight had been lifted off his shoulders.

That time Duncan enjoyed himself. But even then it was a complicated, tiring, and above all noisy adventure, more trouble than it was worth.

These episodes—the joke on the doctors and the New Telford nothing store, eccentric in themselves—point up Duncan's firmness of character, and it was this firmness of character which was to cause him endless trouble.

Duncan lived quietly in his mansion in New Islip with his widowed mother until he was six years and fifteen days old. The morning Duncan was preparing himself to enter his sixteenth day plus six years of life, his mother, Mrs. Jasmine Fitzmorris, appeared in his room, a glass of castor oil in hand.

"Duncan dear," said Mrs. Fitzmorris, "drink up, it'll do you good."

"Not a chance," said Duncan. "I'd rather starve for a year than drink that awful stuff."

"Very well," Mrs. Fitzmorris said flatly. "You won't get anything to eat until you've drunk this glass of castor oil."

Mrs. Fitzmorris was a lady of strong character and kept her promise. Whenever Duncan asked for something to eat, she waved the castor oil under his nose. Duncan resisted for three days; then he stuffed all his toys into a suitcase, fled to Daisy Street, and moved in with his uncle Philip Fitzmorris, who loathed his sister-in-law and adored his nephew.

Duncan lived with his uncle Philip from that time until he was twenty-seven. Then he said, "Unc, I think I'd better go on home now, I've been away too long."

Duncan went home and knocked at the door. Mrs. Fitzmorris came out: she'd aged somewhat in the twenty-one years.

Her right hand was wrapped tightly around the glass of castor oil.

"No, Mother," said Duncan, shaking his head.

Mrs. Fitzmorris slammed the door in his face and let him know what she thought through the window: "You won't set foot inside this house until the day you drink that castor oil!"

Duncan knocked again a couple of times, with the same result. He sat in front of the door for three days. Then he gave up and went back to his uncle Philip.

He lived three more years with Uncle Philip: then Uncle Philip died with a smile on his face.

"Duncan," said he as he expired, "bless you. You've been a delight in my old age and you've saved me the trouble of drawing up a will. Thanks to you, my books are perfectly balanced. After the doctor and the funeral, I will have about half a pound left. It's all yours. Do anything you want with it."

Duncan stayed with his uncle to the bitter end and then distributed the half pound among some charities and found himself flat broke. But he hung around the Daisy Street house for a few days. After a week he received a telegram from the family lawyer: "On the way to Stratton your mother died of apoplexy. Be present at reading of will.—Dickson."

Duncan showed up in the lawyer's office and the seal on the will was opened. It was very short: "To my son Duncan Fitzmorris I leave all my worldly possessions on the condition that he drink, in the presence of my lawyer Herman Dickson and the two witnesses indicated below, one glass of castor oil."

The lawyer, having read the document, called in the witnesses, took the glass of castor oil out of the safe, and handed it to Duncan.

Duncan shook his head.

"No," he said softly, but with great determination. Then he walked out.

Duncan Fitzmorris was a man of character above all, and then one has to take into consideration that after twenty-four years the castor oil had turned green in its glass and was thick as petroleum.

"In any case," the lawyer called after him, "whenever you want it, it's here." And he put the castor oil back into the safe.

This happened at 4 p.m., May 13, 1905. At 4:30 Duncan took quick inventory of his own worldly possessions and decided that to provide for his future he had about a hundred dollars and a couple of trunkfuls of elegant suits. There was merely the matter of the hotel bill. So, having received Clotilda Troll's letter at 7 p.m., Duncan called the porter and said, "Have the bill made up and send a carriage round to take me down to the harbor at eight o'clock sharp tomorrow morning."

After all, he didn't find himself in normal circumstances. Otherwise he would have thought twice about vague invitations to yacht cruises and little kisses from Clotilda Troll.

Clotilda, the rich, eccentric, wild Clo that young and old in New Islip made cow eyes at, had always seemed a clumsy, extremely irritating little girl to our hero. Yet in this particular situation a cruise on Miss Troll's yacht could be a jumping-off point for a glorious future. One thing often leads to another.

Duncan cringed at the thought of marriage, and not a little at the thought of Clotilda Troll. But between a clumsy millionairess and the twenty-four-year-old glass of castor oil, Duncan found marriage the lesser of two disasters.

This is to explain why, upon hearing the discreet knock at his door, Duncan Fitzmorris was very pleased.

"Come in," said Duncan, getting up and tossing his cigarette butt through the porthole.

In came an enormous man with a well-tended black mustache and a gold boutonniere on his high-collared jacket. Even taking stock of Clotilda Troll's not infrequent lapses into eccentricity, this personage absolutely could not be Clotilda Troll.

Evidently he was the captain of the yacht. "Would you be good enough to follow me to our parlor?" the captain said, and Duncan acquiesced, nodding his head toward the door. After all, it was proper that Clotilda Troll hadn't come down to Duncan's cabin, rather had asked him to come up to the parlor, and Duncan, although he was no friend to convention, understood.

Inside the parlor, Duncan found himself in the presence of two young men he'd never seen before, neither of whom could be Clotilda Troll. Duncan didn't make an issue of it. He merely nodded to both.

There followed a few moments of silence. Then the captain deposited a letter on the table. "As you can see, the envelope is addressed to Messrs. Duncan Fitzmorris, Septimius North, and Barton Clegg. I was asked to bring you together in the same room so that the letter might be read simultaneously by all of you." The captain saluted and withdrew.

Duncan, aside from being a man of character, was a man of exemplary calm. Therefore, before doing another thing, he lit a cigarette and settled himself in an armchair. After a while he turned to the other two, who were still standing around looking rather embarrassed. "Gentlemen," said Duncan, "after what the captain said, introductions don't seem necessary. We all know very well that I'm Duncan Fitzmorris, you are Septimius North, and he is Barton Clegg."

Septimius and Clegg agreed.

"Therefore there is nothing for me to do but ask one of you to open the letter and read it out loud. If, on the other hand, this solution displeases you, I'm perfectly willing to tear the envelope in thirds and each can withdraw to his cabin with his own third."

Septimius shrugged his shoulders but Barton Clegg quickly made it clear that the first was the more acceptable alternative. So he tore open the envelope with trembling hands and read aloud.

Gentlemen,

You will forgive my method, but I assure you this is not the usual practical joke. On the contrary, I am quite in earnest.

Born and raised in New Islip, I love this wonder-

ful city, and to make it prettier and happier year by year, I am prepared to sacrifice anything.

I have induced you three, under the tritest pretenses, to board my yacht, for the sole purpose of ridding New Islip of its three most detestable citizens.

Many will say that you are kind and good, but I absolutely cannot. Not only seeing you and speaking with you but the mere thought of you living in the same city is enough to make New Islip intolerable to me.

There are three million people in New Islip, so this may surprise you—"why we three?" But really it's very simple: there probably are people as loathesome as you hidden somewhere in New Islip, but you, besides being the most loathsome, are also the best known, Septimius North for his unbelievable good luck, Barton Clegg for his literary brilliance, and lastly, Duncan Fitzmorris for his extreme wealth and eccentricity.

The Dolphin will deposit you at my command in a place from which, I hope, you will not return for a long time. The crew has strict orders to thwart any plan you might contrive against my intentions.

Again let me beg your pardon.

> *Yours,*
> *Clotilda Troll*

Clegg dropped the letter and looked at Duncan in dismay. Septimius covered his face with his hands.

"That's all?" said Duncan, looking at his fingernails.

"That's all," whimpered Clegg.

"Fine. Let's take a stroll around the deck," said Duncan, standing up and walking toward the door.

But Septimius jumped up and blocked his way. "Mr.

Fitzmorris," said he, very excited, "really this is most irregular. We must do something."

"I was just about," smiled Duncan, "to take a stroll around the deck. That's doing something."

"I suppose," said Septimius, a little calmer, "that's the only thing one can do. However, I would like to point out that I think this a very poor joke indeed."

Duncan shook his head. "I assure you it's not a joke at all. We really are sailing who knows where, we really will not be coming back to New Islip for quite some time, and it's really in earnest."

"Thank heavens," sighed Septimius, mollified. "I'm not keen for jokes, never have been. Can you imagine, I haven't spoken to my father for three years because he pulled a chair out from under me?"

Duncan approved of Septimius North: a man of character. He liked men of character.

"Not a word since, you know," Septimius repeated. "And we live in the same house. When I have something urgent to say to him, I write it down, even if we're at table. Then I call the butler and ask him to take the note over to my father."

Barton Clegg, who up to that point had been staring dejectedly through the porthole at the ocean, tried to collect himself. "It's dreadful," he sobbed. "Never to see her again, never to smell her perfume, never to be able to send her the sweet poems I composed nights! Oh, how I love her!"

Duncan patted him on the back affectionately. "Console yourself, Mr. Clegg. You'll find another girl."

But Barton Clegg shook his head. "Never!" he shouted, wringing his hands. "Never. There's not a woman in the world like Clotilda Troll."

Septimius's eyes bulged out. "You mean to say you're still in love with Clotilda Troll?"

"Yes, yes, yes," wept Barton Clegg. "I love her more now, even as Petrarch loved Laura more after her death. She's a creature from heaven!"

Duncan patted Clegg on the back again. "Poor Mr. Clegg," he said consolingly. "I understand your dilemma. You're so stupid you probably deserve to marry Clotilda Troll."

That sent Septimius into gales of laughter.

Then somebody knocked at the door. "Clotilda?" exclaimed Clegg, looking hopefully toward the door. Septimius started to smile, and then, seeing Duncan slouched in an armchair in an attitude of complete unconcern, he turned to the porthole wearily and began whistling. Septimius was a likable chap, very observant, but completely lacking in critical sensibility.

2

Once upon a time Septimius had spent six months traveling in Germany. He religiously covered every square inch of it, had a close look at hundreds of cathedrals, rivers, gardens, women, paintings, monuments, bridges, and horses. When he returned to New Islip, Septimius ran into some friends. "Did you have fun? Is Germany pretty?" they asked him.

"I don't know," answered Septimius. "I've got to talk to my father first."

Septimius's father was the exact opposite of his son: he had a very fine critical sensibility, but not the slightest eye for detail. Generally he saw things in overall outline. The best description of Septimius's father is to compare him to a man in a balloon tied to the earth by a mile-long rope. A man in this position can only have a panoramic view of the world, and in order to make him grasp details, one would have to pull in the rope. As a rule, Septimius's father operated with the rope played out to its greatest length.

"What do you think of that?" one might ask him, pointing to a carved cherub atop a baptismal font in Madrid Cathedral.

"Well," Septimius's father would answer, "these southern countries, marvelous."

One would ask him to have a closer look at the thing,

and after a while, Septimius's father would admit: "Actually, all of Europe is quite interesting."

The thing was not to get discouraged, to pursue the subject tenaciously, and bit by bit Septimius's father would eke out the information that Spain was full of beautiful things, that Castile was a unique province, that Madrid was a well-built city, that the Cathedral of Madrid was for the most part admirable, that the interior of the Cathedral was fascinating, that the particular baptismal font was rather nice, but the problem with it was the dreadful little sculpted angel which spoiled the whole effect and one really oughtn't to waste one's time gaping at that sort of artistic atrocity.

There were very few people who were capable of reeling Septimius's father in from his outpost in the stratosphere to discuss the merits of a meerschaum pipe or a bay stallion. In fact, that admirable gentleman spent most of his time formulating philosophical statements, essential syntheses, universal generalities. When you come right down to it, Septimius was the only person who got through at all to his father, and that was because he didn't ask his father to come down to the object, instead he brought it up to him in the aerial form of words.

And the other side of the coin: when Septimius returned from Germany and was asked whether he'd had a good time, if he'd seen anything worth seeing, Septimius had to answer, "I don't know, I'd better ask my father." Septimius, having traveled alone, had seen a thousand things and remembered them in minute detail. Yet he had no idea whether or not they had pleased him or even if he'd had a good time. So he described Germany's flowers petal by petal, its music note by note, its cathedrals stone by stone, making comparisons, stating measurements and proportions, never once inserting his opinion. "Beautiful," said his father from time to time. Or: "Ghastly." Or: "Not bad."

Septimius also described girls he had taken walks with, theatrical spectaculars, the new motion pictures frame by flickering frame, Turkish baths, excursions. "Yes, you did have a good time," his father would say every so often. Or: "Wasn't worth going to. Terrible opera." Or: "You were bored to tears at that concert."

After a while, Septimius was ready to face his friends and tell them that Germany was a pretty country and he'd had a good time, more or less.

"What about the girls, what were they like?" his friends asked.

"I don't know, my father wouldn't tell me," answered Septimius.

This will serve to reveal Septimius's character and make it less difficult to imagine him whistling with his head stuck out the porthole. Septimius, after knowing Duncan for only a few minutes, admired him and decided to trust him completely for sensations, opinions, and convictions. The fact that within two seconds Clotilda Troll might come in through the parlor door left Duncan completely cold. So Septimius felt indifferent about it too.

Barton Clegg, on the other hand, sidled toward the door and, after a pause, turned the knob. Even admitting that Clotilda Troll had no end of idiosyncrasies, there was no way of fantasizing that the seven hairy, semi-naked men armed with grappling hooks and arranged in phalanx behind the yacht captain could possibly be Clotilda Troll.

The captain, civilly removing his cap, stepped into the cabin: "Have you gentlemen decided to do something rash?"

Septimius pulled his head out of the porthole and

looked round at Duncan. Duncan continued to blow smoke rings at the ceiling. "No," said Septimius, sticking his head out the porthole again.

"Are you waiting for a better time perhaps? For instance, tonight when the crew is asleep?"

Nobody answered. Septimius kept whistling, his head out the porthole, while Duncan picked with great interest at a soup stain on his jacket.

"Would somebody please answer me?" said the captain, turning to Barton Clegg, who was staring at him wild-eyed.

"I . . . I don't know," said Clegg, very awed.

Septimius drew his head back inside with disgust and looked at Duncan. Duncan turned away and some more smoke spiraled toward the ceiling. "No," answered Septimius, yawning. "But we would like some ham and eggs."

A broad smile stretched across the captain's face. "I'll have it sent up directly," he said, bowing, and the crew put down their grappling hooks. "In the meantime permit me to thank you for the good will you've shown us by not forcing us to throw you overboard as we'd been ordered to do in case of resistance. Thank you: we will trust you. The word of a gentleman is sacred to us."

The sailors in the gangway threw their caps in the air and shouted "Hurrah!" Then the door was closed and the room was silent again.

Clegg heaved a sigh. "Seamen," he said, sincerely moved, "hard, crude people, but good men."

Septimius drew his head back inside and looked at Duncan out of the corner of his eye. "Good men," said Duncan, his lips pressed into his famous half smile, "good men taking us on a cruise. Who would have tossed us overboard if we'd raised a finger against them."

"To be sure," exclaimed Clegg, "but with what regret, though!"

Barton Clegg, as might be guessed, was above all a man of gentle soul. One night on his way home he was accosted by a coarse ruffian who, knocking him over the head with a club and throwing him to the ground, picked his pockets clean. The ruffian subsequently was arrested and tried. The public prosecutor was very severe with the ruffian: it was a clear-cut case of extremely malicious delinquency and he described the ruffian as a subhuman monster.

Clegg at first said nothing. Then he tried to say something but they wouldn't let him. The ruffian was condemned, but Clegg, after the sentence had been read, turned to his attacker. "Never mind," he exclaimed. "We'll take it to the court of appeals."

When the case was appealed, thanks to Barton Clegg's intervention by retaining several brilliant lawyers, the ruffian was freed.

Several months later, Clegg, again on his way home late at night, felt his head clouted by a dull object and his pockets emptied meticulously. Clegg immediately recognized his assailant: of course it was the ruffian. "Poor thing," he sighed. "In the dark you didn't recognize me and attacked, thinking me a stray animal."

"I knew perfectly well you were a man," asserted the ruffian.

"Then you must suffer from amnesia and it's understandable you don't remember everything I did for you."

"On the contrary. I remember you perfectly well, Mr. Clegg."

"Good," said Clegg with pleasure as he passed out. "That proves memory exists. There are still people who remember their benefactors and recognize them even in the dark."

Barton Clegg was a man of gentle soul. Besides, he was a poet and madly in love with Clotilda Troll.

3

After what happened in the yacht parlor, Duncan avoided his companions-in-adventure. Duncan had eaten his ham and eggs in silence and retired to his cabin to smoke a lot of cigarettes and study the situation calmly. But while he did manage to turn the few cubic feet of air in his cabin blue, Duncan could not keep his usual phlegmatic calm. For the first time in his life, he felt ridiculous. In effect a silly girl had been able to put something over on him: in all probability now, while the *Dolphin* was gliding under full sail heaven only knew where, Clotilda Troll was describing to a select group of her despicable friends the details of the trick she had engineered for the benefit of Duncan Fitzmorris, Septimius North, and Barton Clegg.

The thing that bothered Duncan most was being thrown together with two such insignificant mediocrities as Septimius and Clegg. This was the worst sin Clotilda could have committed. Duncan caught himself pacing back and forth across his cabin: ludicrous, since the greatest distance between two points on the floor was two yards. So a silly girl had destroyed his usual composure: the realization, another novelty in Duncan's life, was enough to make him even more nervous.

It really was shocking. Clotilda, who had always had so little meaning for him that he was only reminded of her existence when he ran smack into her, had barged into Duncan's life and in a flash made him the butt of a joke that would keep New Islip buzzing for years. "When I get back I am going to tear that girl limb from limb," Duncan decided. Afterwards he changed his mind. A Fitzmorris absolutely could not deal that way with women. The upshot was that Duncan on his return had either to find some work or to inherit his fortune.

Finding some work meant offering the world the ignominious spectacle of a Fitzmorris who actually earned his own living. Claiming his inheritance offered Duncan the equally ignominious spectacle of a Fitzmorris humiliating himself by drinking a twenty-four-year-old glass of castor oil. Duncan therefore decided to make no decision. For the moment he had only to bear the fact that the idiot girl had taken him for a colossal ride. He had to pull himself together and regain control of the situation and those two mediocrities whom fate—or rather Clotilda—had thrown into his lap for the duration of this misadventure.

By nighttime, when he went topside to the parlor, Duncan had come through the crisis brilliantly. At dinner he was more than charming.

At coffee, Septimius stood up, visibly embarrassed. "Sir," he said, "seeing that fate has united the three of us in this deplorable adventure, and seeing that making decisions unnerves both me and Mr. Clegg, we have the honor of putting ourselves under your command for the duration. We have elected you our leader."

Duncan was moved. "I accept the honor," he said, pleased. "Better to be wrong following one man's orders than waste time and energy on useless words and then have everybody go off and be wrong on his own account." He finished his coffee and called the captain over. "I'm going to try to find out what our destination is," he explained to Septimius and Clegg, who approved.

"Captain," Duncan began, "are you free to tell us where we get off this boat?"

"Yes, sir," the captain answered. "I have orders to land you at Bess Island, and if the ship keeps on course, that's where you'll get off."

Duncan smiled over clenched teeth. "Perfect," he said. "Our kind Miss Troll treats us with such consideration. She is making sure our little vacation isn't upset in any way. If I'm not mistaken, Bess Island is a tiny sand bar lost in the middle of the Atlantic, completely deserted and miles from any trade route. I hope we can count on your own decency to provide us with at least an umbrella and a shotgun, so we can play Robinson Crusoe."

The captain shook his head. "It's true Bess is off the beaten track, but Miss Troll does have a lovely villa there. She herself lived there for three months last year. The accommodations are comfortable and, if you gentlemen require it, I can leave one of my sailors to serve you."

Duncan nodded his head in acceptance. Then he asked if Miss Troll planned to let her guests live on roots and berries.

"Everything is prepared," the captain said. "We'll give you enough to live on for two months. The villa's cellars are full of wines and liqueurs and preserves. Every two months we'll return with supplies."

"How long is this supposed to go on?" Duncan asked calmly.

The captain shrugged his shoulders. "That is something only the good lord and Miss Troll know."

"I think you'd better limit that to Miss Troll," said

Duncan sarcastically. "The good lord, I'm sure, hasn't a clue. It's hard to believe the good lord, if he knew about it, would allow Miss Troll to put a plan like this into operation."

"If the good lord allowed Miss Troll to descend to earth and bring joy," the captain said, backing through the door, "it must mean the good lord was willing to close his eyes to other things."

The yacht, white as a ghost, glided over the glassy sea and the moon lit up diamond lodes in the fleeting wake of water. At two in the morning, someone called in an undertone to Duncan. Duncan sat up with a jolt in his berth. It was Septimius.

"Sorry to disturb you," said Septimius, "but do you think there's anything to be worried about?"

"No," Duncan replied, lying back and burying his head under the pillow.

"Thanks," Septimius whispered and went back to his cabin to sleep soundly.

4

Duncan spent all of the next day despising Clotilda
Troll. He then spent part of the night loathing her. By
the following morning he was in a position to contem-
plate Clotilda with pure hatred. On the third day of the
voyage, Duncan passed with relative ease from hate to
disdain, and on the fourth day, finally, he had suffi-
ciently regained his presence of mind to think sanely.
If, instead of having fallen into the girl's trap, he had
stayed in New Islip, what would have happened? In the
last analysis, he had to admit, Clotilda had got him
out of a jam and opened the door on an adventure for
him in which he didn't stand to lose a thing.

So Duncan spent the fourth day of the voyage mostly
thinking about the problem independent of Clotilda.
After he devoted a good portion of his energy to forget-
ting the girl, he was able to become indifferent to her
again. Close scrutiny of his circumstances in general had
a calming effect on Duncan: the future presented itself
in the form of a thoroughly engrossing riddle. The
truth is, it's marvelous not to know one day what's going to happen the next.

The fifth day, having exhausted his supply of cigarettes and topics of rumination, Duncan recalled the
existence of Clegg and Septimius. Those two unfortunates had subsisted drearily during the previous four

days: they had limited themselves to staring at the ocean miserably, smoking cigarettes, and attempting hopeless, abortive conversations with the captain. Only toward the end of the fourth day had Septimius found a system to ward off boredom. Chance, more than anything else, helped him along. Septimius, during one of his halfhearted exchanges with the captain, had absentmindedly taken some dice from his pocket and begun to fiddle with them as one fiddles with a watch fob or a key chain.

The captain gazed at the dice wistfully.

The captain had long ago found himself in dire straits. He loved to shoot crap but he couldn't: a captain can't shoot crap with his crew. Septimius, however, was not a member of the crew! Had Septimius, from that longing glance, guessed the secret tragedy of the captain? Say rather he instinctively felt it and, urged on by a mysterious force, offered the captain his dice.

This happened about four in the afternoon. At nine the next morning Duncan entered the parlor to find Septimius and the captain sitting at the table rolling dice. From time to time Septimius would groan. "Captain, it's time to go to bed, I'm sleepy."

During seventeen uninterrupted hours of crap, the captain had lost everything: every shilling he had in his pockets, then his salary for the next sixteen years, then his wardrobe, then his telescope, then his sextant, then the navigation charts. After that, finding himself absolutely destitute, he had begun to shoot for the yacht. The *Dolphin* wasn't his but this didn't make much difference; he rolled for it anyway. He began with a coil of hemp, then a grappling hook, then a sail. They had gotten as far as the rudder, the compass, the shrouds, and the jib. Piece by piece, the captain had gambled and lost everything. As Duncan walked in, the captain was losing the last valve on the boiler.

"What's going on here?" asked Duncan jovially.

"We're just shooting crap to pass the time," Septimius explained, smiling.

The captain stared silently at the table for a moment. Then he slammed his fist down and shouted: "I'll take you on, Mr. Fitzmorris. Five pounds on the table against Mr. Fitzmorris!"

"But . . ." stammered Septimius, embarrassed.

"He has no choice," the captain interrupted. "He's my prisoner and I'll dispose of him as I choose."

Duncan frowned at the captain. "You would dare shoot crap against a man who has been put in your trust by your employer?"

"I'm sorry, sir," the huge seaman whimpered, "but you mustn't hold me responsible for anything I say now. I'm ruined. I've lost everything including this ship, which isn't mine. This—this Mr. North has rolled the dice thirty-six hundred times and hasn't lost once. Don't you see, Mr. Fitzmorris? Three thousand six hundred times Mr. North has shot and three thousand six hundred times in a row he's rolled boxcars. And the dice aren't loaded, I swear to you."

This was how Duncan found out about Septimius's most valuable asset.

As the captain wandered off mumbling to himself, Duncan looked closely at Septimius. "So you can shoot dice thirty-six hundred times in a row and have boxcars come up without fail?"

Septimius blushed. "Oh, my," he said sadly, "you're thinking what everybody else thinks. Even you believe I do something funny to the dice. All right, watch!" The backs of their chairs were slatted. Septimius pulled out one of the slats and handed it to Duncan. "Do me a favor: carve two dice. Here's a penknife."

While Duncan whittled away at the slat, Septimius planted himself in a corner, face to the wall.

"I'm finished," said Duncan.

"Now take a pencil and mark them up like real dice," Septimius said, without turning around.

"Done."

Septimius drew near, scooped up the dice without looking, and threw them against the wall. They fell to the floor: six and six. Ten times he picked up the dice and dropped them on the floor or heaved them at the wall or up at the ceiling, each time with increasing annoyance. And ten times the dice turned up boxcars.

"See?" Septimius said finally. "I can't shoot anything but boxcars. Always boxcars, anywhere, with any dice!" And, infuriated, he picked up the dice and threw them at the door.

At that instant the door was opened by a steward who was bringing up their breakfast on a tray. One of the dice bounced off the doorjamb, dropped and turned up six. The other disappeared. Septimius muttered something and then he and Duncan sat down at table. The hot chocolate smelled delicious and there was no point in letting it get cold.

"This unbelievable luck of yours," said Duncan, "must be quite . . ."

He couldn't finish. Septimius, who was sipping his chocolate, let out a shriek and spat violently. Something clattered over in the corner: though it was dripping with chocolate, there was no doubt it was the other die. It placidly displayed six.

Duncan smiled. "As I was saying," he began again, "this unbelievable luck of yours must certainly have earned thousands of pounds for you."

Septimius's face fell. "Well," he admitted, "I've won thousands, but it's a long sad story. I'll tell you all about it." There was no need, because just at that moment, after knocking discreetly, the captain came in. He was in his underclothes and carried several huge packages.

"Mr. North," he began, "I am a gentleman and honor my word. You won all my cash and I handed it over. You won my clothes. You won my books, my nautical charts, my instruments. So here everything is. My salary for the next sixteen years belongs to you now: here's an I.O.U. You collected the ship, every plank of it, and you are now its sole owner. But with all due respect, I must tell you that I can't possibly work for you. I'm firing myself and the crew. We will retire to the hold and await your orders."

"And the ship?" gabbled Septimius. "Who's going to run the ship?"

"You and your two companions."

"All right. I concede the ship," Septimius sighed. "Take back your job."

"Senseless," the captain observed. "How can I steer the ship without instruments and charts?"

"I'll return the instruments and charts."

"How can a captain have any dignity among his men, commanding them in his underwear?"

"I'll give up your wardrobe. Is that all?"

"How can a man have enough peace of mind to watch the currents carefully when he knows that for sixteen years to come he won't have a farthing! No, it won't do. You and your friends will have to go to work right now, because if you look over there you'll see we're running straight into a storm. I couldn't care less any more; but certainly you must."

"I'll tear up your note for sixteen years' pay!" shouted Septimius, on the verge of tears.

The captain shrugged. "A man without a shilling in his pocket might as well be dead. No. What difference does it make to me if the ship sinks?"

Just then the ship listed violently and they heard the first thunderclap.

"All right, all right, here's your filthy cash!" Septimius yelled, scattering a wad of banknotes across the table. The captain leaped to gather them up and scurried out with all his bundles.

The ship was dancing wildly on the waves. Septimius went into a rage and, seeing the dice on the table, he grabbed them up and pitched them out the porthole. Two seconds later a huge wave gushed through the porthole, drenching the entire parlor. Something rattled across the tabletop and bounced to the floor.

"Boxcars," said Duncan, snickering. Septimius snatched them up and threw them out again, slamming the porthole after them.

At that moment Barton Clegg appeared, very agitated. "We're a couple of miles off Bess Island. We'd better hope this storm doesn't blow up now!"

The captain burst in on them. "Gentlemen," the mammoth seaman bellowed, "there's not a second to lose. In this heavy sea I don't dare enter the island channels. In fact, if my bad luck keeps up, the chances are I'll run the ship aground on some offshore reefs. You'd better take a dinghy to land. Once you get ashore there's no problem. Miss Troll's villa is the only house on the island. Here are the keys. The provisions and your luggage are already stowed in the dinghy."

Duncan, Septimius, and Clegg found themselves in this dinghy a few seconds later being hurled from wave to wave.

"I didn't send any of the crew along, so you could stow more provisions!" the captain hallooed down from the bridge. "The dinghy will be nice for little excursions!" he added.

Duncan, Clegg, and Septimius reached for the oars and began to row as hard as they could while the waves rose higher and higher around them.

The landing on Bess Island occurred twenty minutes later, in this order: first the oars, then a suitcase, then a trunk, then Duncan and Clegg clinging to each other desperately, then the dinghy's rudder, and last, on two parallel waves, Septimius and the dinghy.

"It would seem," Duncan observed after he extracted his head from the sand, "that the captain's idea about not loading down the dinghy with crew and filling it up instead with provisions was brilliant. Thanks to his foresight, we now have at our disposal one tin of meat and the nearly intact wrapper from a can of biscuits."

Before he could communicate his thoughts on the subject, Clegg had to spit out a mouthful of sand. Eventually, however, he was able to put forth this agonized exclamation: "The keys to the villa!"

"We'll break in through a window," said Septimius, finally able to peel off his jacket and wring it out. "The point is, we're all alive and safe. And I . . ." He stopped and fixated with bulging eyes on something shining in the sand.

The two wooden dice: boxcars.

A wave playfully climbed up the beach, wrapped itself around the dinghy, and carted it off.

"I think we'd better go find this villa," said Duncan wisely. "A warm fire wouldn't do us any harm."

It didn't involve a major search. Duncan and his companions trudged up a small cliff and found themselves before a perfectly flat expanse from which projected only two vertical objects: a palm tree and a boarded-up edifice. Duncan started off confidently toward the boarded-up edifice. That had to be Clotilda's villa.

The rain began bucketing down viciously. At any cost they had to get inside the house. Duncan, Clegg, and Septimius worked on all the windows on the ground floor. They pulled and pushed, even tried to pry the boards open with a crowbar which by coincidence they came across lying on the ground nearby. But the solid-oak shutters wouldn't budge an inch from their hinges.

Septimius was an extraordinary athlete: assisted by Duncan and Clegg, he scaled the wall to the second floor and began to fool around with the shutters. Same result. The rain meanwhile belted down more persistently and the wind whistled by menacingly. Streams of sea water, rain, and sweat. The three men looked at each other perplexed.

Duncan let out a sigh. "There's nothing for it but to try the door," he said.

The sight of the thick door, plated and studded with wrought iron, completely depressed them. Septimius, deflated, rested his forehead against the doorjamb and began to sob. The door creaked open.

"There," he exclaimed happily, "it wasn't any problem at all. All we had to do was push it open and walk in."

"However, it would have been more polite of you to have knocked first," came a sour voice from inside. Then a pistol appeared before them, and after that an even less benevolent-looking man. Even though by now it must be very clear that Clotilda Troll was a strange eccentric girl, there wasn't the remotest possibility of that man's being Clotilda Troll. "Hands up," the man ordered.

Septimius's and Clegg's arms shot into the air without a word. But Duncan, with his usual calm, wanted to know something first. "The bullets in that gun—are they properly disinfected?"

"No!" shouted the man, nonplused. Then he growled, "If you want to try them out . . . !"

"I'll take your word for it," said Duncan as he raised his arms.

(It is simply miraculous to be capable of remaining calm when confronted by a genuine brigand. Strange as it may seem, during the very same days that Duncan Fitzmorris was sailing across the Atlantic aboard the *Dolphin,* I was drifting about in the vast Argentine pampas. To recall this distant memory would be most appropriate at this point, since shortly Mr. Fitzmorris will be in New York and there he will experience another thrilling adventure. My digression will reveal the behavior of an ordinary man face to face with evil men and make it obvious—if it's not already—how extraordinary Mr. Fitzmorris's gesture really was.)

A LONG DIGRESSION

This was something that happened to me when I was quite young. I wasn't writing for the papers yet. I was a waiter in Mendoza.

What with brothers and sisters, my family consisted of twenty-five people. My mother, however, insisted that there were only twenty-two of us children. "Louie," my mother would say to my father, "every time the good lord sends me a son I carve a notch on the doorjamb. If it's a girl, I make a little cross. Now you count them up, Louie, and you tell me if there aren't exactly eleven notches and eleven crosses. Eleven plus eleven makes twenty-two, right?"

"You must have dropped one out. Remember, four years ago you forgot to salt the stew."

"I most certainly did not forget," my mother would assert. "That one there, the one with curls on his forehead, does not belong to me."

"That one there with curls on his forehead" was me, of course. My father looked at me and smiled. If the good lord had forged us both from the same mold, my father and I could not have been more identical.

"When I look at that one with the curls on his forehead I see you as a boy bringing me sour crabapples whenever I took sick," my mother sighed, turning to my father. "Therefore that one with the curls on his forehead is not mine," she repeated pigheadedly. "Somebody must have smuggled him in among our own and I only noticed when it was too late. There are twenty-two marks on the door and I see here twenty-three children."

One morning my father made me get dressed, put a suitcase in my hand, took me out to the chicken yard where my mother was scrubbing the laundry, and said: "Say goodbye to your mother."

My mother wiped her hands off on her spotless white apron and squeezed me tight. "I'm as sorry to see you go as if you were my own son," my mother sobbed. "I don't know how I'm going to do without this one with the curls on his forehead . . ."

My father rode with me on the train as far as a harbor town and packed me on board a ship.

"Your uncle Philip," he explained, "wrote me that he needs somebody to help him in his business. Your uncle Philip became a horse trader in Argentina and I want you to make your fortune too. You're the brightest of all your brothers. If you'd been stupid like your brothers, you'd have stolen six hundred rounds from my shell box and sold all or part of them: but I knew it could only have been you, on account of you just swiped the lead from all six hundred and sold that for a good price. So when I took a couple of shots at that bandit Jack, it dawned on me I didn't have any lead. But afterwards I thanked my lucky stars. You aren't dumb and you'll do all right. Your uncle Philip will meet you at the dock. Watch out nobody steals your bag on the boat." My father shook my hand and turned red.

During the voyage I kept an eye on my suitcase. As I got off, I grabbed another for good measure. This put me in Uncle Philip's good graces.

My uncle Philip had made a pile of money horse-trading, thanks to his foxiness. Anybody who buys horses usually pays a certain amount and then sells them for a larger amount. Horse-trading is more or less based on this principle. But a horse is no sack of corn: a horse is a living beast that can break a leg, swell up like a balloon, or turn tail and run, never to be seen hide nor hair of again. Therefore even if you buy some horses for a song you stand a chance of earning nothing at all or even losing money.

Eliminating this risk, my uncle Philip dealt in horses only to the extent of selling them. Marvelous system, but of course not everybody can manage it. You have to have a gift, a nose for it, as they say. You have to be able to spot the best horse in a string and rope him in a matter of seconds. You also have to know how to shoot the ears off a gaucho at fifty yards.

"The good lord said thou shalt not kill. And I don't kill. So I haven't had any run-ins with the good lord. Now if the good lord had said thou shalt not shoot the ears off a gaucho, well, I wouldn't, I'd shoot him straight through the head." This was the sort of theory my uncle Philip developed for me during our rides through the pampas. He was a very strict logician.

"The good lord said thou shalt not steal and I don't steal. I trade. Can it be you're not allowed *not* to sell certain items? No. And if you're allowed not to *sell* certain items, why should you not be allowed not to *buy* certain items? He who robs benefits from something that's against the law, right? Well, I don't benefit from cutting the best horse out of a string. If when I first spot the string I have ten cents in my pocket, after I cut out the best bay, I still have only ten cents in my pocket, right? The only benefit I derive from it is much later, selling the horse. That's trading."

My uncle made quite a lot of these declamations to me. But the one that really struck home was the theory of the twenty pesos. "If I buy a horse over the counter and resell it, making twenty pesos, am I dishonest? No. That's twenty pesos earned free and clear, according to any chamber of commerce in the world. If I buy the horse for two hundred fifty pesos and sell it for two hundred seventy, I would then be an honest dealer. But having paid nothing for the horse, if I sell it for twenty pesos as I usually do, why should I be called a thief? My theft is no longer thievery, because instead of robbing two hundred fifty pesos cash, I immediately renounce those two hundred fifty pesos, being an honorable man. The twenty-peso profit represents merely my just due as a trader."

Anyhow the story I want to tell happened while I was in Argentina serving as a waiter in Mendoza.

One day my uncle Philip left me a note tacked to the door of the house:

For a couple of years it'll be healthier if I set up shop some place else. Meanwhile you'd better keep away from the big cities too. One of those confounded gauchos has made things a little difficult for me. Whilst I was shooting at his right ear, he turned profile and the bullet hit his right ear, sure enough, but not before it went through his left too. Watch out for those gauchos! As you can see, they're dangerous.

So I hotfooted it out to the pampas and after I'd gotten far enough away from home, I took a job so as not to starve. At that time it wouldn't even have occurred to me to write for the papers. I swallowed my pride and sweated it out.

I got into trouble, of course. Being a naïve boy, almost a baby you might say, I evidently didn't have the know-how to carry it off. Thus it was that, with really touching ingenuousness, I offered to sell the third horse I had stolen back to its rightful owner. The only thing that saved me was my youth. Today I couldn't possibly get a horse to rear like that nor could I shoot a gun out of the hand of a murderous rancher at forty yards in one try. Oh youth, pure and innocent, when your eyes are clear and your mind calm! How would I ever be able to shoot a gun out of anybody's hand now? I'd need at least a double-barreled shotgun and a whole sack of shells.

I started to wander across the pampas and in my heart was growing an intense hatred for horses, those stupid beasts that had created so many problems for my poor uncle Philip and now were making still more for me. I gave my bay to an old man who, taking advantage of my distraction, ambushed me with a rusty pistol. Sheepishly I handed over my revolver, my gunbelt, and the few pesos I had tucked away in my boots. But he wouldn't take my hat because it was too tight for him.

I ate whatever I could lay hands on and slept on the ground behind thickets. Once in a while I'd run into a tramp and we'd walk a ways together. I remember one night something odd happened to me. I'd lain down for a snooze in the middle of some dense bushes and had been asleep for about half an hour when I heard some thrashing around and then a sigh of relief. Somebody had dropped down to rest a couple of yards away from me.

"Who's there?"

"Misery on the hoof," an ancient but kindly voice answered from behind me.

"Comrades, then," I said laughing.

I heard a sigh.

"You wouldn't have anything vaguely resembling tobacco, would you?" I asked.

"Not a whiff."

"A crust of bread? a sip of brandy? a drop of water?"

"Nothing," my unknown companion sighed.

"Then let's start a partnership," I laughed. "We'll pool our resources. Divided by two, that makes nothing."

"I have nothing. You at least have your youth, and that's no mean possession." My invisible companion sighed again. "How on earth do you come to be tramping about on the pampas in the style of old bums like me?"

"All because of a bunch of mangy horses. If horses didn't exist I'd be in a nice comfy bed right now reading the newpaper."

"You can read?" my unknown friend asked with surprise and admiration.

"Sure. I can write too. Can't you?"

"Not a word. But what's your problem with horses?"

"I came to Argentina to help my uncle run his horse-trading operation. Horse-trading ruined my uncle. I tried horse-trading on my own and here I am, down to my socks, in rags, flat broke. If I ever get off this plain, I'm going to enlist in the navy for life. At least there I'll never see another horse again!"

"I don't know about that. What's going to pull the boat along?"

I started to laugh. "My dear old friend, where were you born?"

"Here on the pampas. I've always lived here."

"That explains it. Born here, lived all your life on this godforsaken plain where nobody sells anything but horses, where men don't even know what it's like to walk any more because the minute they're born somebody sticks them on the back of a horse, where the only things to do are raise horses, break horses, trade horses, steal horses, where lovers ride under their sweethearts' windows on horseback, sweethearts elope with their lovers on horseback, and it seems as if nothing in the world can exist detached from the back of a horse or without being in some other way related to horses. What a blessing the whole world isn't infested with the monsters!"

The old man sighed. Apparently he liked to sigh. "If you ever told a gaucho his horse was a monster, he'd shoot you on the spot," the old man noted.

"Then it's lucky gauchos are an insignificant minority in the human race. In any case, I'd shoot first."

"Young people are usually so crazy about horses. I don't understand what's wrong with you."

"But I already told you: horses have always brought me a pack of trouble."

"Horse-trading is what got you into trouble, not horses. Therefore you should hate trading, not those poor beasts. It's a sin to speak ill of a horse on the pampas. Gauchos when they die need to have their horse in the room with them. The dying gaucho's only question is, What's the sense of going to heaven if I can't bring my horse along? And when the gaucho's soul leaves the room, nobody can see it, not even the priest, who can talk directly to God. But the horse sees it and whinnies in farewell. Horses are not monsters. A horse has a soul like you, young man."

"I think," said I, laughing, "there isn't a gaucho in the world with a soul, but soul or no soul, I wouldn't be about to whinny if I saw one flying out of the room."

The moon had risen and the plain stretched off toward infinity, bare and clear as an enormous yellow table. I heard the branches rustle behind me: my invisible companion had stood up.

"Good night, young man," he said, leaving the thicket's gloom. I turned around to look at him.

It was clear as day, and I swear to you I saw him not more than two yards away. Before moving off eastwards, he stopped for a moment and turned his head. "Good night, young man," he said to me.

He was a horse.

That gave me a scare, but nothing compared to the one I got, speaking of brigands, while I was working, as I mentioned before, as a waiter in Mendoza. Anyhow, I was a poor urchin, an innocent, naïve boy whom fate had carried away from home and deposited in that desolate land.

As soon as I arrived in Argentina I began working, as I've already said, for my uncle Philip. Then Uncle Philip had to make himself scarce and I was left in the lurch. After that I wandered like a mongrel dog across the pampas, trudging along day and night, and eventually one fine day I found myself at the foot of Aconcagua. Aconcagua is an enormous mountain. I'd never seen a mountain that high before. The sun had long since set when I found myself in its southern foothills, but there was no mistaking it.

Bear in mind I was a poor young man and hadn't yet begun writing for the papers. Now I write for the papers and I know the precise height of every mountain on the face of the earth. Then, however, I didn't know that the peak of Aconcagua is 22,834 feet above sea level. But I was very curious to know how high it was then, and fate was quick to help me find out because shortly I stumbled across a hut in which an old man was boiling some milk. I asked the old man how high Aconcagua was and he told me. He also told me that information would cost not fifteen but twenty pesos and, my pesos in his hand, he led me to a narrow path which would take me to Chile without having to cross the Upsallata Pass. He was a very intelligent old man, and before he went back to boil more milk he returned my twenty pesos. A man of the world grasps things quickly and has no difficulty understanding that a poor abandoned boy is much more attached to his only twenty pesos than he is to any of the six bullets in his revolver.

I arrived in San Felipe by train purely by chance. After plodding along for about six hours, about two in the morning I was very cold and, gathering up some dry branches, I lit a fire. The engineer of a passing train spotted my bonfire dead ahead on the tracks and brought his train to a halt to see what was going on.

"What luck!" said I. "Must be fate, this train stopping right where I lit that fire, just as I'm about to bed down. It'd be a shame to let one of those nice berths go to waste!"

I arrived in San Felipe while it was still dark and found a hayloft and slept for a while longer.

The next day I started walking again. I had no idea where I was going, but luckily I came across a man in a cart.

"Where are you going?" I asked.

"Wherever I feel like going," said the man.

"Fine," I answered. "I'll come along."

There was a huge trunk in the back of the wagon, but the two horses were in shape and kept up a good pace all day. The next morning we set off again and by sunset we could see the Pacific. I helped the man drag the trunk down to a small inlet where a steamboat was waiting. The trunk was hoisted on board.

"Everything all right?" the captain of the ship asked.

"Everything's perfect," said the man.

The captain had the trunk opened. Inside there was a man neatly bound and gagged. The trip must have shook him up some, but as soon as the gag was removed and somebody gave him a slug of brandy, he got his strength back and shouted *"Caramba!"* The gag was quickly tied on again.

"You hear that voice?" the man asked the captain. "You can tell a good one by the voice."

"Two thousand," the captain offered.

"Twenty-five hundred," the man replied.

"The last one you brought us wasn't worth a centavo," the captain pointed out.

"That shows you didn't know how to handle him," the man protested. "In Santiago everybody was after him."

"Twenty-three hundred," the captain said, "and not a peso more. Bear in mind he doesn't even have a uniform."

The man pocketed his money and we trekked back to the wagon while the boat steamed out of the inlet.

"Uncle Philip," I asked him as the horses began to gallop, "what became of horse-trading?"

"That went by the wayside," said my uncle Philip. "Now my business is armaments. I sell generals to the Mexicans. There are three or four civil wars every year in Mexico and they lose all their generals. Here in Chile, though, we don't have any civil wars and the generals are thick as flies. It's hard work, but it has its rewards: you have a clear conscience. The good lord hasn't put out any commandments against selling Chilean generals to the Mexicans, has he? Never seen anything about that in Scripture, have you?"

I'd never seen any references to Chilean generals in

the Gospels. I told Uncle Philip so and he seemed very pleased.

"Now if I ask a tailor to make me up some suits, or a gaucho to break some horses for me, is that a sin?" continued Uncle Philip. "No. Therefore what's wrong with asking a general to fight a war? Tailors make clothes, gauchos break horses, generals fight wars: isn't that somewhere in Scripture?"

"No, that's not in Scripture."

"That's a shame," he said, quite upset. "Because it's certainly written that we all have to earn our own bread by the sweat of our brows."

"That *is* written in Scripture," I agreed. "But Mexico's one thing and Chile's something else."

"And isn't it written in the Gospels that all men are brothers?" Uncle Philip insisted gravely. But that didn't convince me.

"Well, yes, in effect we all are brothers: but you only sell generals to one side in these Mexican wars. Aren't the other side also our brothers? Why do you help only one side if the others are also our brothers?"

Uncle Philip drew the cart to a halt and looked me square in the eye.

"I know perfectly well how to interpret divine law," he stated. "I play no favorites. For me all men are brothers. I sell generals to the other side as well."

So I helped Uncle Philip in his armaments business.

My uncle Philip was a saintly man: honest, hardworking, devoted to his profession, but unfortunately he had not an inkling about international protocol. So it happened that one time he shipped to Mexico an English general who was passing through Valparaiso, and a nasty diplomatic incident began to brew. A convoy of British warships turned all their guns on the gubernatorial palace of Valparaiso.

For this reason my uncle Philip had to take a powder and again I was left in the lurch. I was then but a poor, ignorant, naïve boy: how could I continue to capture these important generals on my own?

So I looked for work: all jobs are honorable if they're honest. I played at being a barber and a railroad worker: but ever since I was very little I've always had an independent streak, and so, determined to work in a business I could really call my own, I became a bootblack. The initial costs of becoming a bootblack are negligible and you only need a little money to buy the necessities: a folding stool for the customer to sit on, a little bench to put his foot on, a couple of brushes, a rag, a can of black polish, one of clear wax, and a horse.

I was a poor urchin, a mere boy with no knowledge of life, but it didn't take me long to figure out that the element indispensable to any shoeshine kit is a horse. Few bootblacks get rich, and this is because they don't grasp that the truly essential thing to their trade is a horse. Bootblacks as a rule are nearly as stupid as gauchos: they will plant themselves on a street corner and wait for Lady Luck to put some client's foot under their brush. Lady Luck has other things on her mind and I caught on quickly. To thrive in the bootblack business you have to have quick wit and a horse: quick wit to realize, for example, that if a water main breaks in a certain area of town and the streets turn to mud, the bootblack who installs himself in the immediate vicinity of the unexpected mire is going to do a land-office business. The horse serves to escape from the aforementioned neighborhood in a hurry.

I'll admit my first experiment of this nature didn't come off so well, but it wasn't really my fault as much as Lady Luck's, who flooded a street down by the docks and sent me for my first customer a Canadian sailor just off his ship. Well, I was a poor urchin and hadn't experienced the attitude of Canadian sailors toward bootblacks. The typical Canadian sailor will sit down on the stool and wait for a bootblack to finish shining his shoes. Then he will kick out both legs and send the bootblack flying across the street. Then, thumbs hooked into his belt, he goes swaggering off down the sidewalk.

Being a poor urchin with little knowledge of such things, when I felt the Canadian sailor's feet resting on my forehead, to keep from falling over backwards I grabbed the first thing that offered itself to my hands. As luck would have it, that happened to be the handle of my revolver. On that unfortunate occasion, the horse was very useful to my bootblack business.

But the anecdote I'm driving at had nothing to do with my being a bootblack in Valparaiso. That business in Valparaiso was something else. My business prospered and I worked with joy, moving from east to west whenever my sense of smell told me to.

One day, when I was working around Cabecita Street where a water main had just exploded, a little man wearing glasses and sporting a goatee sat down on my stool. He was a chatterbox: never in my life have I heard such a lot of idle ranting. Immediately he told me that times had never been this bad and the worst of it was happening in Valparaiso. He rattled off a whole slew of incidents.

"You've got to keep on your toes," the little man said. "There are really some bad types running around loose in Valparaiso. All you have to do is look at the papers. For example, there's that hoodlum, nobody knows what his name is, who goes round doing all sorts of dreadful things. Did you read about him, boy?"

"No, sir," I replied.

"You should, dear boy. More fun reading what he's

up to. One day he took a forged letter over to a barber on Santa Cruz Street that said his wife was very ill. I'll watch the shop while you run home, says our friend. Soon's he's alone, he puts on a white smock, and when a man comes in, he lathers up the man's face and starts in on shaving him. Just as he begins to work on the fellow's chin, there's the blade against his throat and the poor fellow knows if he doesn't get out his money there's going to be the devil to pay. So, wallet in hand, our friend fills the man's mouth with lather and walks out, calm as you please.

"Another time, he gets on a train, puts on a conductor's cap and goes round collecting all the passengers' tickets because, says he, they have to be validated. At the first stop, a mile from Valparaiso, he gets off minus the conductor's hat, has his horse brought round (he'd shipped it up the day before), trots back to Valparaiso, installs himself in front of the train station and begins to tell the story how he'd bought passage to this or that place, how he couldn't go now and would gladly sell the ticket to anybody headed that way. So one by one he sells all the tickets!"

"What a fascinating fellow!"

"Curious, yes," the little chatterbox went on. "Really a curious chap. You know what they say he does for a living?"

"No, sir."

"He's got quite a system, that one," said the little man. "It seems he arrives in a certain place, cracks open a water main to inundate a portion of the street, sets himself up as a bootblack nearby, and waits for someone to get his boots dirty and come to him to have them shined."

"Must do a whopping good business!"

"A fantastic success because, when the opportunity

arises, the fellow puts down his brush, grabs the client by the heels, and leaps up. Then the customer falls over backwards, his shoes come off in our friend's hands, and, shoeshine kit tucked under his arm and already mounted on his horse, he gallops off and nobody's ever seen him twice."

"How strange!" said I.

Then, dropping the brush and grasping the little man's feet tightly, I leaped to my feet. As on all the other occasions, his shoes came off in my hands, but this time the customer didn't fall over backwards. So I had to abandon my shoeshine kit as I jumped on my horse, my heart pounding. I will swear it on a Bible, I saw it with my very eyes: that little man not only wasn't wearing any socks but he had two cloven hooves. So I was a poor urchin and I'd lost my shoeshine kit. But I had managed to steal the shoes straight off the devil's own feet.

That was the second scare I had, but it was nothing compared to the business of the Mendoza brigand. We'll have to let go of these Chilean reminiscences and go back to Argentina to get right to the point.

You've already heard once or twice that I was a poor urchin, one of twenty-three brothers and sisters—twenty-three little fish swimming around in the milk of life —that destiny was playing out on a line and allowing to wag its tail through the turbulent waters of the oceans. After my uncle left me high and dry in Valparaiso, I returned to Argentina and wound up in Buenos Aires. It was a horrible trip, as I recall. At the Villa Mercedes stop, a track repairman came along the freight convoy tapping the rails with a hammer and forced me—by knocking me over the head with his blasted tool—to relinquish the nice spot I'd found under the caboose, and there I was, halfway between Mendoza and San Luís.

There's nothing less wise than to set a bad example for a young boy. A young boy is encouraged to imitate the actions of his elders, to recognize them as infallible experts on life. For this reason it's not so odd to find that a boy, having just been knocked over the head with a hammer by a grown person, decides the only just course is to hit the man back with a similar metal object, and, finding myself revolver in hand, I belted the trackman's forehead with the handle of my gun.

I was a poor boy with holes in my shoes and my clothes in tatters: let us agree that a boy ought to know how to deal with things as he finds them, and who would accuse me of improprieties when on that occasion, having found a perfectly decent jacket, a serviceable pair of trousers, two fine boots, and a nice cap left lying there on the trestle, I gathered them up and put them on? Nevertheless, there had to be somebody who'd find it scandalous that a poor young man in a railroad repairman's uniform took to traveling clinging to the underside of a freight car, and then set up a great clamor. But fortunately this happened only a few miles outside of Buenos Aires during a stop on the open plain. In such circumstances the only solution is to make a run for it and take a dive into the tall grass.

There's nothing worse than twilight on the pampas. Loneliness sets in with a vengeance, and try to find your way out of that tall grass. From time to time you feel the dried-up bones of some horse's skeleton crunch under your boots and you think, "Maybe in a couple of months a gaucho'll come along and trip over me the way I did this horse."

I walked for nearly half an hour. Then divine providence gave me back my faith in life and I came across a living creature. It was a young gaucho who, squatting in front of the door to a hut, was playing a guitar. Seeing me all dressed up as a railroad worker, he snickered and asked me if I'd missed my train. That was about the stupidest thing anybody could have said under the circumstances, and for that reason nobody but a gaucho could possibly have said it. Granted, gauchos are beings of an incredibly low intelligence, but I've never seen any as asinine as that one. He kept snickering and asking me if I'd missed my train, while he coaxed out of his guitar the most ear-splitting yowls imaginable.

Which prompted me to tie my jacket over his head with the help of his guitar strings. I wandered off, after rediscovering that a gaucho's horse is, if anything, stupider than its owner. This brings to mind the tale of the medieval donkey whose words of wisdom ought to be whispered in the ears of every horse in the world. A horse was fleeing the onslaught of the enemy and came to a halt beside a donkey who was calmly munching on some grass. When the horse asked him why he hadn't turned tail the same as the rest of them, the donkey answered: "Better to wait for a new master to come than run along behind the old."

All right, you shouldn't expect a horse on the pampas to know anything about medieval donkeys. According to him, though, he could only have one master: his gaucho. So every time I tried to come near him, he'd prance off into the fields. Night had settled in, and the glow of the lights from Buenos Aires hung over the crest of the tall grass. I was beginning to get chilly and I looked around for something to put over my shoulders.

Now I was a poor urchin without a jacket or a hat. I knew perfectly well that what you found lying around didn't necessarily belong to you, but who's to think badly of my moral principles if, coming across a calf only a few days old, I picked it up and put it over my shoulders? It was soft and warm and smelled of milk.

The story I'm going to tell happened when I was working as a waiter in Mendoza, but the calf incident is relevant because it throws light on something that happened to me in Mexico. By the time I got to Buenos Aires it was late at night. I wandered through the half-darkened city until I ran into a mean-looking character who wanted to know what I was doing with a calf wrapped around my neck. Then he wanted me to tell him all about myself and come with him to God knows where.

We resolved it by having him follow me: but even with a calf over my shoulders I could run faster than he could. Then I found myself trapped in a small square and, seeing an open gate, I slipped through it. I spotted a ladder and climbed up to a landing where there was another stepladder. After another four of these ladders I wound up in a small but quite airy little room. Noticing that beneath me the city of Buenos Aires stretched out on all sides and above me hung a cluster of bells, I decided I must be in a bell tower. I slept in the belfry and at noon the next day the bells woke me up. The calf was gazing at me lovingly.

I stayed for quite a while in Buenos Aires, and providence helped me out by finding me a number of jobs. I even made a little cash but I never moved out of the bell tower in the chapel of Santa Maria. I would leave home at dawn and come back late at night. I built myself a soft, comfortable cot and there I kept my scanty savings. Every night I brought the calf milk, oats, seed-cakes, chocolate, and a large jug of water. The little square below was almost always deserted except when a little man arrived on the run every day around noon to give the bells a tug. I loved that man like a brother and cherished him as one cherishes a good-luck charm.

I stayed a long time in Buenos Aires and everything went well. But one afternoon, following a hunch, I returned to the bell tower and found the little square jammed with a howling mob. Whatever had possessed the calf to climb up and hang out the window in the belfry? There it was, its forelegs draped over the parapet, looking down with a satisfied smirk on its face. It was definitely asking to have its ears boxed.

Meanwhile the crowd was shouting "A cow in the belfry!" In two years (you don't pay attention to these changes day by day) a calf of the female sex turns into a fair-sized cow; and mayhem breaks loose in a crowd because they can't figure out how a cow can climb a ladder, much less fit through all those narrow trap doors. Everybody was quite upset: when finally the bravest one made it up to the belfry with a cup of holy water and came across my cot, and under my mattress found a mass of watches, gold chains, silver plates, and banknotes, the people were informed and fell to their knees in awe, having decided that the good lord meant to punish this vandal who had terrorized Buenos Aires for two years and had ensconced himself in the tower of Santa Maria by turning him into a cow.

I was still a poor young urchin, so I started to cry: not so much at the loss of my small nest egg as to see the most honest cow in all of Argentina being maligned and treated like a thief. It was impossible to get the cow down through the trap doors and someone suggested she be butchered up there. But then a loud voice warned them that if she had once been a man, one had to remember one couldn't cut men up without trying them!

After shouting this, I left, but I had the consolation of seeing my cow lowered from the tower on an ingenious system of ropes and pulleys. What became of the poor creature? Did she wind up in the slaughterhouse or in prison? I don't know.

The run-in I had with the brigand happened while I was a waiter in Mendoza: the melancholy story of the calf is relevant only to explain why, finding myself in the vicinity of a farm near Orizaba and having to choose between a calf, a piglet, and a chicken, I chose the chicken without a moment's hesitation: this species of animal never gets very big and therefore no sizable troubles follow in its wake. The calf, the piglet, and the chicken were all three shut up inside crates, but I felt most sorry for the chicken. While the other two animals' crates were quite ample, with nice wide gaps between the slats and no tops, the chicken was locked up in a niggardly little cage with tightly spaced slats on all sides.

I freed the chicken from its prison and by and by, when an uncouth farmer approached me to register his disapproval of my action, I easily made him see the light. It's amazing how simple it is to find arguments for the cause of freedom. Seeing as I was a poor urchin, an innocent creature of God, it was hard for me to put two words together most of the time, but when it came to fighting for the cause of freedom, I always managed to muster enough eloquence to make the most boorish farmer understand that if he didn't go away immediately and let me alone I would willingly sacrifice every bullet in my gun for the cause.

But this incident involving Chiquita the emancipated hen blew up in my face. I must therefore announce that I was no longer in Argentina but in Mexico and that I had arrived in Vera Cruz from Buenos Aires by a miracle. If I hadn't immediately dived into the ocean when the captain of the *Martin Garcia* discovered me under the canvas of a lifeboat, and if I hadn't been able to swim like a fish to the not-too-distant coast of Mexico, I might never have found myself in the environs of Vera Cruz. And, let's be frank, it was also a miracle that I found myself on Mexican soil decently dressed. If, in fact, divine providence hadn't meant for me to throw myself into the sea, how could I possibly have come upon a beach, presented myself to the eyes of the world as a mild-mannered person just back from a long swim, entered the most promising-looking cabana (after careful study of the situation from a nice sunny spot on the sand), to emerge from it shortly thereafter, impeccably dressed?

Here again we have a poor urchin, a minnow hooked to the line of fate in the stream of life and tossed into the turbulent oceans to swim for it, only this time on Mexican soil. I wandered up and down through the highlands: in the big cities there was a lot of shooting going on. One of their frequent short revolutions was just coming to an end, one of those little tiffs that give the Mexicans, who have no enemies in the outside world, ample opportunity to make as many as possible among themselves. It's truly remarkable how, in those days, the Mexicans felt a strong need for enemies and how I, on the other hand, felt the need to avoid making any.

I drifted around alone like a dog and one morning found myself in San Luís. It was market day and I strolled through the mob of Indians inebriated with the sun and pulque. At one point a man drove up in a cart heaped high with yellow grass. The cart was drawn by two horses and he was riding one of them. He stopped right in front of me and told me to watch out for the horses. Some Indians loitering nearby glanced at the grass and shrugged their shoulders. A gentleman dressed in a white suit and a broad panama, holding a parasol in his left hand while fanning himself with his right, walked straight up to the cart.

The cart driver approached him. "Sir," he said, taking off his cap, "would this load of hay be of any use to you?"

The gentleman scrutinized the hay and then shrugged his shoulders as the Indians had done. But the cart driver didn't give up easily. "Sir," he persisted, "do me the favor of listening, at least. I need money very badly. If you won't buy the hay, at least buy my cart. I'll throw the hay in for free."

The gentleman began to look at the cart with more interest. The cart driver lifted a corner of the heavy blanket of hay, some of which straggled down to the road, then pointed to a set of wheels and gave their spokes a couple of sound taps with his knuckles. "Mister," he explained, "it's really a bargain. I need the money and I'm selling everything."

The gentleman scribbled an address on a bit of paper. "Bring this rattletrap around to my house and unload it. Then we'll have a look and maybe we'll make a deal."

The cart driver told me to come along and help him unload the hay.

We arrived in a sunny courtyard. The gentleman in the panama hat was waiting for us. I helped the cart driver unload his hay: the gentleman watched us carefully, then offered a sum of money. The cart driver made him a counteroffer but after a while they agreed.

Outside the courtyard the cart driver mounted one of the horses and I the other, and as soon as we got out of San Luís the horses broke into a gallop.

"Uncle Philip," I shouted after him, "how long have you been selling cannons?"

"Ever since I became a sergeant in the artillery," my uncle Philip explained.

"What side are you on?" I asked. "General García's or General Zurillo's?"

"Well, a little on one side, a little on the other. Until yesterday I was in García's twelfth regiment and sold that equipment here in San Luís, which is on Zurillo's side. Now I'm going over to Zurillo's twelfth regiment and I'll sell their artillery in Hidalgo, which backs García. Then I'll go over to García's thirteenth regiment, then Zurillo's thirteenth, and so on."

"Are there very many regiments left?"

"Six on each side," said Uncle Philip cheerfully. Then he reined in his horse and looked me square in the eye. "You haven't by chance read anywhere in Scripture where God prohibits men from exchanging 77 millimeter cannon between partisans?" he asked gravely.

Now I was a poor young man and I wasn't yet writing for the papers, but I knew Scripture by heart. I answered no: the good lord never made the vaguest allusion to cannon in his declarations on Mount Sinai. Uncle Philip seemed very pleased. "As long as you follow divine law you'll never get in trouble with human law," he assured me. And we started to gallop again.

The event I want to tell you about happened while I was a waiter in Mendoza, not dealing in artillery with my uncle Philip. My uncle Philip, in any case, again left me in the lurch very shortly, because through a perfectly excusable lapse on his part he tried to sell a Zurillo cannon to the Zurillists instead of to García's men and had to take off at a gallop. That was when I freed Chiquita the Orizaba chicken, and having to keep us both hidden well away in a dingy little inn (where somebody brought me food at ninety pesos a meal: otherwise the Zurillists were going to be informed of my presence), I taught her how to hop along on one leg, do somersaults and any number of marvelous tricks.

After the two generals passed by the wayside, I came out of retirement and joined a traveling circus. What else could I do, poor urchin that I was? It was a three-ring traveling circus with elephants, a bearded lady, an acrobat, a ballerina, famous acts, and of course the people were clamoring to get in.

My act made a big hit with the chic circle who were able to spend three pesos for a front-row seat. Nobody else could see the chicken but they applauded heartily anyway. After she'd been through her steps, I'd pick Chiquita up and carry her around, showing her off to the people in the first and second rows. The ladies and gentlemen would hold out centavo pieces and Chiquita neaty collected them in her bill and tucked them away in my coat pocket. It wasn't a bad act at all and everybody liked it.

But one night there was a great to-do and Chiquita walked out on me forever. As the audience was leaving the tent, one of the ladies from the front row set up a howl. She must have been the wife of some bigshot because shortly thereafter the place was lousy with police who were rounding everybody up. The entire audience was questioned before anyone could go home. They frisked us too and turned everything inside out. They even went so far as to cut open the bars of soap.

There were at least eighty coppers and they really threw the place into an uproar. Nobody managed to find the diamond, though. The lady had worn it hanging round her neck on a gold chain: somebody evidently had snipped one of its links. The diamond—

worth ten thousand pesos—had disappeared. And it was during this hubbub that poor Chiquita died. Well, I was a poor young man, an innocent creature who'd always done everything God ordered me to, who lived from hand to mouth, so you can't possibly blame me for what happened. But, to tell the truth, Chiquita's death was a little my fault. Whatever made me, as we were doing our rounds along the front row, ask Chiquita to swallow that tripe?

I was just a boy, and, as we all know, boys are restless and don't have the patience to sit back and let nature take its course. So that same night Chiquita was forced to give up the ghost. That was how I found, salted away in Chiquita's innards, the diamond which had caused all the hullaballoo. Then I roasted Chiquita and ate her. But my heart was full of bitterness afterwards.

I swear to you, gentle reader.

The nostalgia for those serene days of my youth has kept me off the subject far too long and it's made me forget I'd set out to demonstrate—by showing how an ordinary man behaves face to face with brigands—the true beauty of Mr. Fitzmorris's composure. What I'm talking about and what should interest the reader happened when I was quite a lot younger and wasn't yet writing for the newspapers. I was a waiter in Mendoza.

I arrived back in Argentina from Mexico, God knows how. Naturally my uncle Philip had left me in the lurch again. So I was a poor young thing, an innocent boy, and I wandered around for months on the pampas, desperate, barefoot and starving to death, seeing nothing but gauchos and horses. Finally one day I came across a sign of civilization: train tracks.

I staggered along the track bed for a couple of hours without spotting a living creature. Then, coming around a curve flanked by a wall of dense brush, I ran smack into a crew of men working on the tracks. There were five of those filthy gauchos. But a well-dressed man with a railroad official's cap on his head was ordering them around. This cheered me up: it meant they weren't common brigands.

As I arrived, they were just finishing up. After ten minutes the railroad official took some books out of a briefcase, wrote something down, and gave each gaucho three pesos. It was dogs' pay. Those five unfortunates had laid nearly half a mile of track, reaching as far as the banks of the Paraná River, complete with switch. Railroad companies pay extremely poorly in Argentina: even so, the five gauchos mounted their horses and galloped away, perfectly happy with their three pesos and waving their sombreros at the official.

When we were alone, the railroad official asked me what business I had being in those parts.

"It's a free world," I answered firmly. "It doesn't all belong to the British Railway of Argentina."

We chatted for a while, then the official mounted his horse and rode off at a gallop. Meanwhile night had fallen: I sat down dead tired beside the switch to the spur. The minute I heard the train whistle I threw the switch handle. A wagon chugged past slowly, quietly left the main line, and rolled off down the spur. The railroad official was sitting in the brakeman's seat regulating the speed of the car.

I threw the switch handle back in place, hopped on the horse following the car, and trotted along behind. The car rolled very nicely down to the river bank, where a sturdy-looking barge was moored. Evidently there was a piece of track fastened to the deck of the barge and connected to the spur's track. And in fact the car did roll right onto the barge and come to a halt. The railroad official clambered down, wedged a couple of blocks under the wheels to keep the car from rolling, started up the barge's engine, cast off the lines, and we moved into the river's current.

"Is this hard work, Uncle Philip?" I asked as soon as we were in the middle of the river.

"No," my uncle Philip answered as he worked the tiller. "But it's complicated. The railroad helps me quite a lot by leaving stacks of ties and track lying around, and even labor isn't very hard to find. These stupid gauchos would build the Transsiberian for three pesos. The only dangerous thing is jumping from horseback onto the last freight car and uncoupling it. Once it's uncoupled, the job is done: you can pretty well control the speed of the thing, and at a good gallop you can beat the car to the siding switch. But you've got to remember to pull the switch back where it belongs. Otherwise you'll make a mess of things."

At midnight the barge glided alongside a small dock where some men with wagons were waiting. They emptied out the freight car. Uncle Philip counted the money and said it would do. Then we boarded the barge again and midstream my uncle Philip pulled out the blocks from under the wheels and, after a brief hesitation, the freight car rolled off into the water.

A little further downstream, Uncle Philip made his usual sage observations. "The good lord said thou shalt not steal, and I don't steal, I work for the railroads. Maybe it's a sin to build railroad sidings? You with all your education: did you ever read anywhere in the Old or the New Testament that thou shalt not construct railroad sidings?"

There you are: neither in the New or in the Old

Testament is there the slightest hint about railroad sidings, and for this reason I had to go along with my uncle Philip's logic.

The story I want to tell happened while I was in Argentina but when I was a waiter, not while I was working for the railroad with my uncle Philip. The latter was a shortlived job. One night my uncle Philip forgot and left the switch open and a whole freight train steamed off into the Paraná River. There weren't any casualties because the crew knew how to swim, but the accident upset the authorities and Uncle Philip advised me to go west, while he went off to the east.

I must ask you to keep in mind that I was only a boy and I didn't even have dreams about writing for the papers. Now of course things are quite different. Now I do nothing but hand over typescripts to an editor and everything's in perfect order. To be sure, I arrived here in irons, but the irons were attached to boots. How could I possibly have presented myself to a publisher then, when I arrived in Mendoza, with no boots at all? Then I was a poor waif, a creature of God cast off in a savage land, all alone without any job to speak of. What could I do in Mendoza except work as a waiter?

The truth was I went into Don Pedro's café just for a cup of coffee. Don Pedro gave me the evil eye as soon as I sat down at one of his tables, but he brought over a cup of coffee and a basket of bread. Then I called Don Pedro back.

"How much?"

"Eighty-five centavos."

"Well, sir, if you'll give me fifteen centavos, I'll owe you a peso."

Don Pedro groped around in his pockets and handed me the fifteen centavos. "Here: now go back to the kitchen and wash up the dishes. Then come out front again and do the windows. Then go down cellar and polish the bottles I've got stored there."

That night when I came up from the cellar I was hungry and the fifteen centavos bought me a coffee and a couple of rolls. I slept on a park bench, and the next morning around eight I decided to look in at Don Pedro's. I asked him if he needed a waiter.

Don Pedro shook his head. "Sorry, boy, I already have a waiter and I can't send him away just so I can hire you."

I was only a poor urchin at the time and the small irritations of life that make me smile now made me quite nervous then. I left very perturbed and walked along staring at the ground. Good lord, how can you blame a poor little boy, hangdog and barefoot? Let's agree: a poor waif who walks hanging his head could blindly run into you and knock you down: but that's no reason to get angry with the fellow, is it? You shouldn't call a poor boy walking along hanging his head a bad name just because he butts his head into your stomach and flattens you.

A man was flattened and called me a very crude name, thereby offending my mother's family and at the same time maligning the animal kingdom. Nobody will accuse me of ill will if I defended my family and the honor of dogs.

The man went off, both eyes black, and even today I feel some remorse.

"You're a lucky fellow," said Don Pedro. "My waiter sent a message that some hoodlum jumped him and he won't be coming to work for three days."

For three days I was the eagerest and happiest of waiters. Presentably dressed and washed up, I'd never been a bad-looking chap, and Don Pedro's oldest daughter even pinched me a couple of times.

The fourth morning there I was again, unhappy and wandering around hangdog in the neighborhood of Don Pedro's café. Where is the heartless man who will gainsay a poor young boy who, sincerely wanting to work but finding himself on the dole, walks around with his head hanging and accidentally smacks into a fellow? After all, I was still a boy and I was beginning to miss my father, my mother, and my twenty-two brothers and sisters who were so far away. You shouldn't ever call a boy in this state of mind bad names. The boy will react violently, defend his honor, and begin to flail his arms around like a windmill. I saw the man totter off drunkenly. My heart aches even now when I think about it. But why did he call me that name?

When Don Pedro saw me walking past the front of his café, he called me in. The waiter had sent someone to say that he'd been jumped by a hoodlum again and wasn't able to come to work for five days. Divine providence was giving me a hand. I worked for five days, happy as a lord.

On the sixth day, there I was again, skulking around Don Pedro's with my head hanging. Believe it or not, again it happened that I bumped my head against a man's stomach by accident and again I was called a bad name. Now what could the people of Mendoza have had against me?

I swung at him like a madman, crying all the time, poor abandoned boy that I was. The man ran off screaming. But this time divine providence stepped in firmly. Don Pedro was beside himself with rage. He shouted he'd had it with these stories of hoodlums jumping his waiter and then trying to break his neck. The same story three times was too much. He was fed up with these lying drunkards. He didn't ever want to see that worthless waiter again.

"I'm taking you on steady, boy," said Don Pedro, and, thanks to divine providence, friend to poor abandoned lads, I'd found a job.

What I've been driving at all along happened to me precisely while I was a waiter in Mendoza. Boys adapt very quickly and soon I was settled and happy in Mendoza. The customers tipped well, so I was able to buy myself a good suit and some shiny new shoes. I rented a small but comfortable room. I worked all day long and wasn't free until midnight; I had a good time anyway because I made some entertaining friends with whom I cheerfully spent the hours between midnight and three o'clock. One night we'd play dominoes, another we'd chat, a third we'd take walks in the moonlight.

Being a boy, I'd never known what real fear was: anyway, while I was working as a waiter in Mendoza I had the worst scare of my life. In those days the people of Mendoza spent a lot of time talking about somebody named Chico. You heard about him everywhere, even in the newspapers. Chico and his gang were the terror of the Mendoza rich people. As they came out of the theater or left a café, every shadow was Chico to them. The police patrolled the streets every night in vain. They'd set up hundreds of unsuccessful ambushes. But if the police were uptown, Chico and his gang were downtown, and vice versa.

I'd never worried much about Chico when I went home at midnight. In fact I'd never even thought about Chico, or if I had, I just shrugged my shoulders. I was just a boy: what difference could Chico make to a mere boy? Chico was a problem only for rich people with fat billfolds. So I'd always gone home whistling merrily. I'd never been afraid.

One night as I was locking up the café I noticed there was still somebody at one of the tables. I'd never seen the fellow before: middle-aged, rather plump.

"I'm closing up, mister," I said.

"You're closing up already?" he asked, turning pale.

"It's midnight: even I have to go home sometime. I live all the way over in Puerta do Sul."

"In Puerta do Sul? You go home to Puerta do Sul every night?" The stranger was astonished.

"Sure, I live in Puerta do Sul. I'd be an idiot if I went to Puerta de la Paz every night just because it's closer."

"What about Chico?"

I started to laugh. Chico meant nothing to me. Chico couldn't possibly be concerned with waiters.

The stranger got up and moved closer. "You're a silly boy," he exclaimed. "Chico is a desperado and these desperadoes don't split hairs."

"But Chico, from what I hear, doesn't murder people."

"Who knows? It's no problem to make a body disappear. If you ask me, Chico's the most dangerous criminal of the century."

This stranger must have been scared out of his mind, and nothing is more contagious than fear. He confessed to me that the mere thought of having to walk home alone in the dark drove him into a frenzy.

"I just know it!" he whimpered. "Tonight I'm going to run into Chico. I'll give you twenty pesos if you'll walk home with me."

I accepted but, I must admit, without much enthusiasm. I was a mere boy and I'd never known fear. In any case, walking out of the café behind the stranger, I noticed that my heart was beating faster than usual.

We walked in silence for a ways. Then suddenly the

stranger grabbed my arm. "Look over there," he gurgled.

Something was moving in the shadow of an alley. I swear I had an almost irrepressible urge to turn tail and run, I don't know why. I pulled myself together: I'd never been afraid in my life! Then in a flash I felt a shiver run up my spine. What if this stranger . . . What kind of comedy was this, anyway?

After what seemed like hours the man whispered, "We're here." He handed me some money. "Wait a minute," he begged me. "Wait until I get inside the house. If you hear me yell on the stairs, come running."

I gave him my promise. I'm a man of honor, so I swear to you, the minute I heard his door close, I ran like the devil, ran like a madman, clawing at the wind in my face, my teeth clenched, sure that every stray breeze was Chico's hand, that bandit Chico, or one of his gang grabbing me around the neck.

I found myself sweating and exhausted at Puerta do Sul. I was terrified I'd find Chico lying in wait for me in the short alleyway up to my house. I tiptoed along with my heart in my mouth and slowly pushed the door to my room open.

I saw a bunch of evil-looking men sitting around. "Hi, Chico," the mugs said.

"Hi," I answered.

All right. So Chico was me.

Now you've seen the fear inspired in an ordinary man by brigands and desperadoes. It's a dreadful thing that only somebody who's felt it can tell you about. I'm willing to swear it: William H. Bonney was the same person as Billy the Kid, but I'll bet you William H. Bonney was terrified of Billy the Kid. Even though they were the same person. So imagine the fright you'd feel when it was actually somebody else! Which all goes to show what impressive strength of mind Mr. Duncan Fitzmorris demonstrated face to face with the desperado who'd appeared in the doorway of Clotilda Troll's villa on Bess Island.

5

Duncan and his shipmates, after walking through a foyer and a parlor, found themselves in a large kitchen lit up by the glow from a fireplace. A dozen men were sitting round the fire. That gloomy bulk of forms installed between our protagonists and the rosy warmth of the fire could certainly elicit no cheery thoughts from our friends.

"Surprise, Bill," said the brute with the revolver.

An oil lamp brightened up the room. The men rose and moved towards Duncan, Septimius, and Clegg and frowned at them in silence.

"Excuse me," said Duncan with his usual calm, "but we're not used to this sort of treatment, and holding our arms in the air like this is most fatiguing. Now if you don't mind . . ."

A dozen pistols thrust out menacingly at the three men.

"The first one of you who moves gets shot!" shouted Bill.

Septimius, impulsive as always, snickered. "That's a stupid thing to say," he said.

"Like I told you, the first one who makes a move gets it!" Bill shouted.

"All right, we're agreed on that point," Duncan interrupted serenely, "but since we're not allowed to move, as you've so delicately informed us, is there any reason why we shouldn't talk?"

Bill obviously wasn't keen for this sort of conversation. "Cut it out!" he ordered explicitly.

"You're quite right," Duncan agreed. "I shall cut, as you say, it out. It seems in very bad taste to go on. You can tell your employer that her joke went over like a lead balloon. Now I'd like to dry myself off, if you don't mind."

Saying this, Duncan lowered his arms and walked confidently over to the fireplace.

"You put up your hands and stop playing the hero," Bill raged. "Otherwise you're a dead man."

Duncan, settling himself in an armchair, raised his hands and observed: "I can understand about an old, senile man like the captain of the *Dolphin,* but it's a shame to see healthy intelligent men like you lending yourselves to the idiotic pranks of a stupid young girl."

Somebody entered the room and a woman's voice floated over Duncan's shoulder. "You mean to tell me I'm nothing but a stupid young girl?"

Duncan didn't bat an eye and answered with his usual calm. "Exactly. If you are Miss Clotilda Troll, you have the distinction of being a stupid young girl."

"Stand up," the woman's voice ordered.

Duncan stood up, turned around, and found himself face to face with the most important, most alluring, and most mysterious blonde in the world. Duncan lowered his arms again and bowed very politely.

"Please accept my apologies," he said. "I'm a victim of a dreadful misapprehension. A lady named Clotilda Troll played a practical joke of questionable taste on us. She tricked us into boarding her yacht, made us land —or rather tried to sink us—on this island, which according to the yacht's captain belongs to Miss Troll.

We were supposed to remain in this villa until it pleased her to let us return to the world. I thought these gentlemen were hired by Miss Troll to liven up the joke. Either we're on the wrong island or Miss Troll hasn't got an island."

"No," the delightful blonde answered, "you're on Bess Island all right, and this villa belongs to the Trolls, but these men weren't hired by Miss Troll to make her joke any funnier. Quite to the contrary."

Duncan bowed again. "I understand perfectly, miss. Taking stock of the fact that the villa belongs to the Trolls and that these men therefore inhabit a house that doesn't belong to them, not to mention their guns, their appearance, and the way they treat people, I feel that I can say with some degree of certainty that I find myself in the presence of genuine outlaws."

"Aren't you clever," the blonde said.

Duncan raised his hands again. "I think that now is the time to conform to their wishes." He turned to Bill. "You'll forgive my sarcasm, Mr. Bill, but you understand the mixup."

"It's none of *my* business," growled Bill. "She's the boss."

Duncan shook his head sadly. "It must be fate, my life always being at the mercy of some woman or other."

"You can put your arms down now," the girl said. "All of you."

Septimius had been asleep for about an hour on a couch in the foyer. Barton Clegg, his eyes popping out, was standing in a corner with his arms stretched above his head. He was paralyzed with fear. Nobody could get him to lower his arms: the men tried to pull them down, to no avail. They were like cast iron.

Finally Bill pulled out his revolver. "Put down your hands or I'll shoot!" he shouted.

At last Clegg lowered his arms.

The beautiful blonde, lounging in an armchair with her legs comfortably crossed, had lit a cigarette and was watching Duncan absentmindedly as he busied himself in front of the fireplace with his now steaming clothes.

"Kitty," Bill said in an undertone, "what are we going to do with them?"

"Who are they?" she answered, yawning without looking at him.

"Frisk them!" Bill ordered his men, and Duncan's, Septimius's, and Clegg's wallets were handed over to the beautiful blonde. Kitty looked through the cards and papers carefully and had a long whispered discussion with Bill.

Then Bill approached Duncan. At first he was a little embarrassed but then he managed to blurt out: "I apologize for taking you to be Feds, but you know, you've got to keep your ear to the ground these days, Mr. Fitzmorris. Now don't you want to let your families know you're safe and sound?"

"It's nice of you to offer," Duncan answered, "and we're very grateful."

"Yeah," Bill went on. "The wife and kids would probably be glad to hear you're okay."

"If I had a wife, your suggestion would be very apt, but fortunately that's not the case."

"Okay, okay," Bill said, getting impatient. "You can write to your parents then. For example: 'Dear Ma and Pa, I'm safe now, but if you ever want to see me again, you got to hand over with no questions $200,000 to the bearer of this letter. Your loving son, et cetera.' Get the point?"

"Absolutely, and if you were to take the letter to my

parents personally it would give me intense pleasure."

"How do you mean that?" asked Bill.

"In the sense that both my parents are dead. Anyway I'm the one to whom I should be writing these letters."

Bill looked at Kitty questioningly and then exploded at Duncan.

"Look here, bud, let's put our cards on the table. You're the only one of these creeps who has the nickels, and Kitty knows that for a fact, she's had a gander at your papers. Now you're going to shell out for all three of you, and if you don't want to start breathing water, you'd better cough up the two hundred G's in a hurry. We need the dough for a little project. We're keen on taking a little junket over to New Islip."

Duncan shrugged his shoulders.

"So sit yourself down and write your banker or your lawyer or something. On account of if you don't fork over two hundred G's it's all over for you and your friends."

Duncan spread out his arms. "I'm truly sorry, but unfortunately in order to get that money I have to go to New Islip myself. My mother passed away only a month ago and there are some stipulations in the will."

Bill went off to talk to Kitty and came back.

"So we'll take you to New Islip but we'll hold your friends here as hostages. If you don't come up with the dough, it's curtains for both of them. As you can see, we're willing to meet you halfway."

"I recognize your good intentions, but that's not the only problem. For me to inherit this money I have to drink a glass of castor oil my mother tried to force down me when I was six."

Bill clenched his fists. "Now let's stop with the games," he hissed. "We're not going to sit round here forever while you give a floor show!"

Duncan calmly told them the story of the glass of castor oil and concluded: "Believe it or not, that's the way things are. Therefore, I'm terribly sorry, but I can't accept your proposition."

"How do you mean that?" grunted Bill.

"I mean, rather than drink that glass of castor oil, I'll willingly sacrifice not only my own life but those of these two kind gentlemen with me."

Septimius had been awake for a while now and he and Clegg wedged themselves into the group around the fire.

"I don't mean to contradict you," Septimius observed timidly, "but this aversion of yours to castor oil seems to me to be a little irrational. You have no idea what good a glass of castor oil can do for you."

Barton Clegg agreed. "If you only knew the exquisite verses the castor plant inspired in a Chinese poet of the fifteenth cent—" he stammered. But Duncan wouldn't let him finish.

"A Fitzmorris always has the last word," he insisted gravely. "The most disgusting business in the world to me is trafficking in opium, and if you asked me to choose between death and opium smuggling, I'd prefer to die. And if tomorrow I had to choose between smuggling opium and drinking a glass of rancid castor oil, I'd smuggle opium."

A moment of pregnant silence. Then Kitty's voice. "If I understand the gist of what you're saying, Mr. Fitzmorris, I think I should tell you that as a matter of fact we are opium smugglers."

Duncan bowed, smiling. "I'm not surprised. Considering this gang is run by a woman, I'd expected something even worse."

The deluge continued. The gang's jaws were stiff from yawning. After a few hours they'd begun to ignore their three prisoners completely. Clegg and Septimius, stretched out on sofas, were sound asleep, and Duncan had almost gotten his clothes dried out.

The first memorable event of the day occurred at a quarter to four in the afternoon. Rolling over on his sofa, Septimius let the two wooden dice he'd picked up on the beach fall out of his pocket. When they stopped spinning, they naturally turned up boxcars. The rattle and whiteness of the two infernal cubes caught Bill's eye from where he was sacked out nearby. Bill was in much the same situation as the captain of the *Dolphin:* he loved to shoot crap but he couldn't play with his men. Kitty was adamant on the subject. A second-in-command should never put himself in the position of having to draw a gun on his own men for gambling reasons.

Bill shook Septimius awake.

This happened at 3:45. At 4:45 the huge room looked like this: fire in the background, in front of which Duncan (warming his hands); a couch to the left, on which Clegg (asleep); in the center of the room twenty smugglers (in a tight circle piled on top of one another). In the middle of the circle a table, in the middle of the table a pair of dice which, for the eight hundred twenty-sixth time, showed up boxcars.

Nobody said anything any more. Bill was gaping at the dice which, as Septimius rolled them, continued to turn up boxcars like clockwork. By ten of five Bill had lost every penny as well as all his men's money. The gang was stone broke. Septimius's pockets were bulging with dollars and pound notes. When the last of the gang's money was off the table and into Septimius's pockets, there was a moment of pregnant silence. Then Bill jumped up and pulled out his gun.

"Reach for the sky and haul out that dough!" he intoned hoarsely.

Septimius, after pleading a little, heaped the banknotes on the table. They left him a penny.

"Now then, let's start all over again," said Bill.

Another hour and another eight hundred forty consecutive boxcars on Septimius's part and there was the gang, cleaned out again. Again Bill's gun under Septimius's nose. How long was this going to go on, Septimius's hands in the air while Bill pulled everything out of his pockets except the one penny?

At the end of the eighth round Septimius was exhausted. Bill punched him, picked his pockets, and left him the penny. Septimius clenched his teeth, tensed his muscles, and rolled the dice. Snake eyes!

After turning up boxcars 6,311 times in a row, Septimius had rolled snake eyes. You could have heard a pin drop. Up shot all twenty guns.

"You cheated!" Bill screamed fearsomely, stuffing the barrel of his gun into Septimius's mouth. Septimius blushed and hung his head, and then began to roll boxcars again.

Night passed and another ugly day began. Around noon Bill approached Duncan and, hand on his revolver, informed him: "Until you write that letter, none of you get fed."

"That's all right," Duncan answered. "We'll die of starvation."

"How do you mean?" asked Bill, squinting his eyes.

"I mean you're never going to see that two hundred thousand dollars."

"You're a pain in the neck," Bill muttered.

Duncan, Septimius, and Clegg spent the entire day yawning. Also all night. Toward noon the next day, Bill came over to Duncan and announced that Kitty wanted to have a word with him. Duncan took his time but went up to the second floor and knocked.

Kitty, blond as ever, was sitting in front of a table heaped with food and bottles and eating with gusto. "How are you, Mr. Fitzmorris? Have a chair."

Duncan sat down and crossed his arms.

Kitty ate quite a lot. From time to time she described her palatal experiences to Duncan. "Let me tell you, Mr. Fitzmorris, how good this caviar is . . . I find bottled partridge superior to freshly cooked, don't you? . . . You know, ham when it's cured like this is exquisite."

Duncan nodded knowingly.

Finally Kitty couldn't stuff any more down and looked across at Duncan. "Would it be brash of me to ask if what you've just seen has made any impression, Mr. Fitzmorris? I'm perfectly willing to offer you this sort of entertainment again tonight, tomorrow lunch, tomorrow dinner, ad infinitum."

"I'm always willing to see something of this nature, in fact I consider myself fortunate to be able to watch such a lovely mouth and teeth used to such good advantage. If I weren't afraid of being indiscreet I'd ask you to start all over again right now."

Kitty got up and began pacing. "I'm really curious to see if today, tomorrow, the next day, for all eternity if you want, you'll be able to keep up this cheek," she said after a while. "I do think that in a couple of days the sum of, say, two hundred thousand dollars won't seem such a high price for a meal."

"Two hundred thousand dollars wouldn't, but a glass of castor oil would. I swore I would never put my lips to that glass. And I, Miss Kitty, am a Fitzmorris. Let me tell you a story about a paternal uncle of mine, Colonel William Fitzmorris, who was under siege by the Russians for two months. He and his detachment only had a sack of flour left, and the enemy, aware of this, studied the wind every day to know where to set up their kitchen so the smell of the food cooking would waft inside the fortress's walls. On the thirty-first day my uncle, Colonel William Fitzmorris, sent out a messenger to discuss things with the Russian general, Ostrov. 'My commander, Colonel William Fitzmorris,' said he, 'notes that among the various smells you've sent over, there hasn't once been the odor of fresh bread. He presumes therefore that you must be completely out of that heavenly food or else have had to substitute stale crackers for it. He has taken the liberty of sending me with this bagful of loaves still warm from our ovens.' After he said this, the emissary handed over the bagful of fresh bread. Three days later, although he knew perfectly well there couldn't be a molecule of food in the fort, General Ostrov struck camp and marched off. Miss Kitty, it is impossible to break a Fitzmorris through starvation."

Kitty dropped into an armchair, crossed her legs, and rubbed her head against the cushions. "You're a very interesting man," she said.

"It's also impossible to seduce a Fitzmorris, Miss Kitty; once my great-grandfather . . ."

"It is, however, quite possible to beat a Fitzmorris to a pulp!" snarled Kitty, exasperated. Then she rethought the idea and developed it with more calm: "I mean to say that soon, very soon, we might have to rough you up a little." Even so, her voice low and her eyes half-closed, this was a fairly dire threat. But one should always take what a woman says seriously.

The storm lasted for eight days, and the smugglers' small inboard danced around in the island inlet. At last on the ninth day the sun appeared in a clear sky.

"All right, let's get moving," Kitty ordered.

A few minutes later the men were all packed and ready to go. Duncan, Clegg, and Septimius lugged down the three suitcases full of Mr. Troll's clothes that Kitty had generously bestowed on them.

"What about them?" Bill asked, pointing to Duncan, Clegg, and Septimius.

"They're coming with us. Never a good idea to leave witnesses behind," Kitty explained.

"As far as that goes," Bill said, caressing the handle of his pistol, "there are other ways of taking care of them."

"There are other ways of making certain chatty cretins shut up, too," Kitty snapped.

"How do you mean that?"

"In the sense that the less one hears from imbeciles like you the better."

As the boat chugged off, Kitty and Duncan stood on the bridge and watched Bess Island shrink in the distance.

"Duncan dear," Kitty said, handing Duncan the telescope, "can you make out that little speck over there?"

Duncan squinted through the tube and then handed it back to the girl.

"Kitty, you know what that speck is? That's the *Dolphin,* Clotilda Troll's yacht. And do you know what the other speck dressed in white on the captain's bridge is?"

"Some woman," Kitty said.

"Wrong," Duncan corrected her. "That's Clotilda Troll."

6

Clotilda Troll, at the time of this story, had for the past twenty-five years been the richest and most beautiful girl in New Islip. She was also the most eccentric woman in New Islip, but this only for the last twenty years, because during the first five years of her life, Clotilda had given all indications of turning into the most normal human being on earth. The very night of her fifth birthday, Clotilda insisted she wanted Josephine in her bed instantly.

Mr. Troll began to laugh and Mrs. Troll thought her daughter's demand was most peculiar. Ten minutes later, Mr. Troll, who was wandering around in the garden, heard himself being called and raised his eyes to spot Clotilda, lit up by the moon, perched on the roof, her feet dangling over the rain gutter into thin air. Mr. Troll, Mrs. Troll, the governess, the secretary, and the entire staff got down on their knees and begged Clotilda not to budge until the fire department arrived.

Clotilda promised not to move a muscle until the firemen arrived. She also promised that as soon as they arrived she was going to jump.

Mrs. Troll and the female portion of the staff promptly fainted. Mr. Troll sent word to the fire department that under no circumstances were they to leave the station, even if they came to be surrounded by fires. Then he began bargaining with Clotilda.

"When you tell me Josephine is in my bed, that's when I'll come down."

It was no easy job getting Josephine up the stairs to Clotilda's bedroom, but they finally managed it. It was much more difficult to tuck her under the sheets. This in the end called for violence and the use of thick ropes. In any case, that night Clotilda slept alongside Josephine, the oldest and most venerated cow on the Trolls' dairy farm in New Telford.

This natural tendency toward eccentricity was much aggravated by Clotilda's uncommon firmness of character. For example, the day Clotilda turned six, Mr. Troll had a rude shock.

"Clo," Mr. Troll asked his daughter that morning, "why don't you ask that nice boy Louie over to play sometime?"

"Over moy dead body," said Clotilda. "He's the ugliest little pig Oy've ever set eyes on. Besides, it's a bloomin' soight more fun hangin' round with Charlie's kids at the docks. There ain't a game they don't know how to ply."

Even though it's hard to put New Islip harbor slang into print, it didn't take much to convince Mr. Troll that his daughter's language was that of a New Islip stevedore. Naturally he was appalled and hastened to correct the situation. Very shortly thereafter, an imposing linguistics professoress arrived, wearing a pince-nez. She had more letters after her name than a university chancellor. "Your daughter will not allow any expressions to pass her lips but those endorsed by the Academy of Linguistics of New Islip!"

Seven days later the imposing professoress held an audience with Mr. Troll to give him a progress report on his daughter. "Your kid's doin' all roight! Oi'm cleanin' up her ruddy langwij bit ba bit, but blimy, wot a rough toim she give me them fusst few dies."

A week after that, anybody who wanted to talk to the noted professoress had to visit Charlie's Pub down at the piers. Enthroned behind a table in this very popular New Islip harbor tavern, at all hours of the day this estimable and oft-kudoed lady held court, feather hat cocked daringly and a pipe in her mouth, carrying on hours of animated discussion with the stevedores. Such was the strength of Clotilda's character.

By the age of twenty-five, Clotilda Troll was not only the richest, most eccentric, and most beautiful girl in New Islip, but also the most dangerous, since, being as she was frightfully rich, she could permit herself to put into action any and all of her peculiar ideas. To tell the truth, there were so many of these extremely unconventional ideas popping into Clotilda's delightful head all the time that the better half of New Islip hated her. The other half of New Islip consisted of the men, who of course worshipped Clo. Barton Clegg was head over heels for her. The only man who wasn't in love with Clo was Duncan Fitzmorris. And this wouldn't have been quite so bad if Clo weren't . . .

But this is running too far ahead. The thing is to proceed at an orderly pace. Let's go back to the morning of May 20, when, just back from Bess Island, the captain of the *Dolphin* presented himself to Clotilda to tell her what had become of the people she had given him charge of. Clotilda was avid to know about them. "So?"

"Everything went fine, Miss Troll. Three showed up, three debarked."

"What did they say?"

"Nothing much: Mr. Clegg recited some very flattering poetry about you. Mr. North was a bit annoyed because he couldn't figure out what you wanted to send him to Bess for. That's all."

"What about the third man?"

The coarse sea captain fingered the cap between his hands uncomfortably. "Well, Mr. Fitzmorris did point out that he wasn't very keen for what was going on. In fact, he even said some rather disrespectful things about you."

"And then?" asked Clotilda.

"Then he did nothing but sleep and eat heartily."

"The landing went all right?"

"We have reason to believe so. Mr. Fitzmorris and Mr. North are excellent swimmers and certainly they would have been able to reach shore without leaving Mr. Clegg behind. Although the boatswain did tell me Mr. Clegg began to stow a lot of water almost right away."

Clotilda leapt to her feet. "What's this? What's this?" she said.

"It was all that hurricane's fault," the captain began. Then he told her about the rather hurried debarkation of the three men. When he'd finished, Clotilda ordered him to ready the ship. Then she yanked the bell cord and told her maid, who scampered in, "Go to Georgie's. Tell him to pack up and come here instantly with his cases."

7

It wasn't long before Georgie showed up, impeccably dressed for travel and puffing like a walrus. Georgie was an extremely fat man with a small mustache and a few stray hairs running across his scalp. To compensate for these defects, he was very elegant and flat feet did not detract from his natural dignity.

The minute she saw him, Clotilda threw her arms around his neck. "Georgie," Clotilda sobbed, "I'm so unhappy!"

Georgie very politely expressed his opinion. "Clo, was it absolutely necessary, I mean truly, for me to get all dressed up to travel and pack a couple of trunkfuls of clothes just to be told this? I mean, wouldn't it have done for me to come just as I was, that is, perfectly decently dressed?"

Clotilda broke away from Georgie brusquely and began to yank all the service cords in her bedroom. Seconds later a considerable number of servants were scurrying madly through the corridors of the Trolls' town house, some looking for dresses, others for trunks, still others for hatboxes.

At times like this, Jacob the butler stationed himself in the middle of the green room, the point of intersection for all this activity, and directed traffic to avert unpleasant accidents. And as soon as the senior Trolls heard the racket of the bells, they would flee from the green room, in summer to the terrace, in winter to the furnace room in the cellar.

Georgie's reserve, in these situations, became the purest passivity. He would sit in an armchair and wait without raising a finger, without uttering a syllable, his mind a complete blank. Only once had he ever opened his mouth.

"Georgie!" Clotilda had called that time. "Georgie, where are you?"

"In here," Georgie had replied from inside a trunkful of Clo's dresses.

Less than half an hour later, everything was ready, and after a wild rush in the carriage, Clo, the bags, and Georgie were aboard the *Dolphin*. When New Islip was a dozen or so knots behind them, Georgie asked very respectfully where they were headed. Clotilda, hanging out a porthole, drew her head back in and clutched Georgie's hand. "Georgie," said Clo in anguish, "what if they're all dead?"

"What if who's dead?"

"Duncan Fitzmorris, Barton Clegg, and Septimius North!"

Georgie then made one of his statements that so exasperated Clotilda. "So what if they're dead? Once you're dead, you're no longer alive, and that's that!"

"You are the most insensitive man I've ever met in my entire life. Haven't you any idea, Georgie, if they're dead, what kind of a mess that puts *me* in?"

Georgie shook his head. He evidently didn't grasp the situation. Weren't Duncan and his friends on some sort of deep-sea fishing junket in the middle of the Atlantic? He was sure he'd read it somewhere in the news-papers. What had Clo to do with fishing junkets?

"Georgie," Clo said with even greater anguish, "Dun-can Fitzmorris and his friends are *not* on a cruise. *I* in-veigled them onto this boat and shipped them off to Bess Island. The thing is, nobody knows if they *are* on Bess Island, because they were trying to land during a squall and their dinghy capsized and that's as much as anybody knows."

Georgie admitted that this was a horse of a different color. But he still couldn't figure out what Clotilda had to do with it all. "Sorry," Georgie apologized, "but I still don't see how you come into it. I suppose you whipped up the squall and capsized their dinghy."

Georgie's logic was one of the real blemishes on the collective character of New Islip. The other two were the sanitation system and the postal system. But the dozens of manholes which blew open every day and the hundreds of registered letters which arrived in shreds or went astray fell in the shade alongside Georgie's logic.

"You nitwit!" Clotilda shouted. "If someone points a revolver at your temple and presses the trigger and you drop dead, according to you, the murderer is not the man but the powder in the shell, which forces a bit of lead to emerge suddenly and enter your brain!"

"Precisely," answered Georgie. "If there weren't any powder in the shell, the man could press the trigger two hundred times and the bullet still wouldn't come out."

Clotilda began to whimper. "Georgie, don't you real-ize, if he's dead, I won't ever see him again?"

Georgie held out his arms to her. "Clo, why are you getting upset with *me*? I agree completely. If he's dead, you won't ever see him again. But weren't those three just the people you most wanted to be rid of?"

"Yes," Clotilda sobbed. "But I'm in love with Duncan."

Georgie went over to the porthole and stuck *his* head out, but Clotilda grabbed him by the sleeve and forced him to sit down again.

"Georgie," Clotilda exclaimed, "why are you making that funny face? If I can't bare my soul to my fiancé, who *can* I talk to? Since when are you so hardhearted?"

"I'm not hardhearted," Georgie protested feebly. "I'm just a bit annoyed that you're in love with Duncan Fitzmorris. After all, you never told me any of this before . . ."

"Georgie, this is no time to begin splitting hairs over questions of form. This is too important. Tell me the truth, do you love me?"

"Clotilda, do you need to ask? What more do I have to do to prove . . ."

"Georgie, you love me and you're suffering, right?"

"Clotilda, I suffer over you, I've suffered the tortures of the rack for you . . ."

"So look, Georgie. What you suffer for my sake equals what I suffer over Duncan. Do you still think it's the time to quibble about questions of form?"

"Clotilda, I owe you an apology. But you must understand, fiancés are usually extremely jealous. However, do go on and confide in me, I'll make an effort."

Georgie had always made an effort. If Clotilda had ever said to him, "Georgie, climb up the flagpole in front of the post office and stay there until day after tomorrow, will you, dear?" Georgie would have climbed and stayed. But Clotilda had never asked Georgie to do that or anything else quite so unreasonable. Clotilda was a spoiled brat, but never in bad taste. A girl who manipulates true devotion to make her fiancé do idiotic things is not only stupid but guilty of bad taste. Clotilda was intelligent enough: knowing that Georgie was completely in love with her, she took pity on him.

"Georgie," she had said to him one day, "you're in love with me and leaping through rings of fire because I'm not in love with you, nor will I ever be the tiniest bit. Therefore you need a good friend to tell your troubles to, so let's get engaged, Georgie. I'll be your friend and try to console you and give you good advice."

And truthfully Clotilda did try to alleviate his misery.

Georgie was all set to go whenever she called. He went wherever she wanted and never mentioned the word love. Still, he was pining away. Clo worried for a while and then one day she got nasty. "Look here, Georgie," she said, "you're tearing your hair out over a girl who doesn't love you and won't ever. Day and night, you're taking this lying down. You're not making the slightest effort. You must do something about it. For example, why not try to forget me?"

"I can't do it. I love you too much," Georgie said.

"You have to try. Why not go out with other girls? I'll help you. I'll introduce you to a lot of girls that are far nicer than I am."

Georgie made himself go out with the other girls. Clotilda helped him in every way. It was wasted effort. Clotilda made him go on tours, learn sports, attend classes, take up painting, start stamp collections. After every experiment Georgie would shake his head and confess, "It's no use, Clo. I'm still in love with you."

This upset Clo very much. She couldn't stand to see Georgie suffering. She'd done more than any woman ever had for a man to help him out. She even described the real Clotilda to him, with no defect omitted. It was no use. "No, Clo, you're not at all like that," Georgie said after she'd finished.

Now in the parlor aft, Clotilda was confiding in Georgie. "Georgie, I am in love with Duncan Fitzmorris. I never told you before, I know, but you mustn't be offended. Nobody else knows. *He* certainly doesn't."

Georgie was confused for a moment. "Clotilda," he said finally, "I can't figure out why you'd be in love with a man and then send him off to Bess Island."

"At the same time that I love Duncan, I detest him. Every man in New Islip would walk through fire for me, would turn purple if I so much as glanced at him. This goes right over Duncan's head. He doesn't even know I exist. Last year at a charity ball one of my kisses was auctioned off for five hundred pounds. When I went round selling lottery tickets for the stray-dog fund, I said to him, Mr. Fitzmorris, one ticket alone costs a pound, a ticket plus a kiss costs two. Do you know what he did then? He handed me a pound note without one word. And that's not all. Two minutes later Mrs. Astor snickered and said, Mr. Fitzmorris, I don't see why you had to be so rude just to save yourself a pound! Then do you know what he said? I wasn't saving a pound, I was saving myself a kiss!"

"He really is dreadful," Georgie agreed. "I'd enjoy giving him a thrashing."

Clotilda began again, more excited. "Now is it clearer what the state of things is? I mean, could any self-respecting girl stop that arrogant clown in the street and say, Gee, Mr. Fitzmorris, I'm in love with you? To avoid the possibility that I might someday do just that, I packed him off to Bess Island. That was supposed to remove the danger for the time being. Don't you see?"

Georgie said he thought she'd done the right thing. But he couldn't understand why she'd sent Barton Clegg and Septimius North along with him. "Don't tell me you're in love with them too?"

"Don't be an idiot, Georgie. Obviously I had to do it. If I'd sent him off alone, Duncan immediately would have known what was going on. That girl's trying to attract my attention, he would have thought. With a wise arrogant smile all over his face. So I sent two nobodies along for the ride. And perhaps now all three of them are drowned," Clo wound up, sobbing, "and perhaps I'll never see that insufferable halfwit again and I'll be forced to throw myself off the post-office balcony!"

"We'll jump off together," Georgie suggested helpfully, a heroic light glimmering in his eyes.

"Oh, Georgie, how can we both be this unhappy!" Clotilda sighed through her tears.

"What if they're alive?" Georgie asked after a bit.

Clotilda stood up and stopped crying immediately. "If that arrogant clown is still alive, I'm going to show him who Clotilda Troll really is!" Then she added, "I loathe him!"

8

The *Jeannette* steamed along all day. Toward nightfall Bill, who was on watch, sounded the alarm and the crew came up on deck. "That scow over there," Bill explained to Kitty, "smells to me like the Feds."

Kitty didn't seem to be worried. She only asked Bill if he'd done what she'd told him to. Bill said everything was taken care of, and everybody went back to their stations. Half an hour later three officers boarded the *Jeannette* and Bill greeted them respectfully.

"Are your landing papers in order?" the inspector asked.

Bill led the three officers into his cabin and showed them a bundle of documents.

"Everything seems to be in order," the inspector said after he had examined the papers. "What is the purpose of your visit?"

"We sail this ship for Miss Kitty Bleecker. The *Jeannette* belongs to her and she pays our salaries. It's all there in the landing papers," Bill pointed out.

"No, really?" the inspector said sarcastically. "I suppose this is Miss Kitty Bleecker's pleasure yacht?"

"Not everybody's got the income of a customs inspector, what with fringe benefits and so on," a voice said with heavier irony. "We simple citizens have to make do on more modest means."

The three officers wheeled around. There was Kitty, very striking in her nautical clothes.

"I beg your pardon, miss," the inspector stammered. "You must admit this shabby-looking tub isn't fit to have a beautiful lady like yourself on board."

Kitty smiled, flattered. "To what do we owe this visit?" she asked languidly.

"We had a tip that a good-sized opium shipment is coming in, and unfortunately we have to search every ship we spot from stem to stern."

"Whatever we can do to help . . ." Kitty made a mock bow. Then she had a wicker chair brought over and sat down with studied elegance.

Three more policemen came aboard. The inspector ordered Bill to assemble the crew with their gear on deck. Duncan, Septimius, and Clegg were pulled out of their cabins and lined up with them.

"What's going on?" Duncan whispered as he passed Kitty.

"Don't say anything I wouldn't say," Kitty whispered back. "Even if they threaten you. Duncan, please don't give me away!"

The inspector called the crew over one by one, examined the portfolio of documents Bill had given him, and checked everybody's passports. Meanwhile his men were searching the boat and the tapping from their hammers could be heard on deck. Not a speck of dust was going to escape them.

After they had covered every inch of the ship, the inspector asked the crew to turn out their pockets. Kitty refused to be searched. Instead she took off her pea jacket, dropped it on the deck, and stood there in a delicious bathing suit.

When he came to Duncan, Septimius, and Clegg, the inspector frowned.

"Is this some kind of joke, captain? You said there were twenty crew. I count twenty-three, if I'm not mistaken."

"These aren't crew," Bill said.

"So who are they? What are they doing on board? Carrying passengers without a license is illegal."

Bill spread his arms imploringly. "Excuse me, but there's no law against saving castaways, is there? Because if there is, the next time I find anybody drowning, I'll let them sink, if that's the way you want it."

"Don't give me any of that stuff. If you pick up shipwreck survivors, you have to log it in."

Bill opened the fat book he was carrying and read aloud: *29 May, 16:30 hours. During a squall over Bess Island, we picked up three people who said they swam to shore after the shipwreck of their craft. Names: Duncan Fitzmorris, age 30; Barton Clegg, age 39; Septimius North, age 36; all of New Islip. Their papers are in my hands and they will be turned over to the Port Authority upon landing.*

The inspector checked: it was all written down the way Bill had read it. He asked Bill to hand over their papers and studied them carefully. Then he nodded. "So you are three castaways?" he asked harshly, staring at Duncan.

"No," Duncan began with his usual monumental calm, "I'm not three castaways. I am *one* of the three castaways you have been speaking about. The other two are respectively to my left and right."

"Hurray!" exclaimed Septimius. "Three cheers for precision, Mr. Fitzmorris."

This complication worried the inspector. "Did these people have any baggage?"

"Three footlockers, right behind them. They were only able to salvage a few personal effects."

"Do those three footlockers belong to you three gentlemen, the ones behind your six legs?" the inspector inquired sarcastically. Duncan, Septimius, and Clegg turned around. There were the three trunks full of Mr. Troll's clothes that Kitty had donated to them on Bess.

"Yes," said Duncan.

"Will you give me your three keys so that we may inspect them, please?"

Duncan, Septimius, and Clegg handed over the keys.

The inspector opened the padlocks, lifted out the trays, and let out an exclamation of triumph. "There's enough opium here to poison the entire State of New York!"

Three jaws dropped in amazement. Even Kitty came over to have a look.

"Oh!" said Kitty indignantly. "This is incredible!"

"And you, Mr. Precise Castaway, what do you have to say about this?" the inspector asked Duncan.

Duncan retained his composure. "Just as Miss Bleecker said, Inspector, this is incredible."

"You haven't much imagination, young man. This is old hat. You land your boat on some beach, pretend to be shipwrecked, get yourself picked up by the first ship that passes by, and very calmly you load on the opium. Isn't that so, my three opium smugglers?"

Duncan shook his head. "Inspector, you're quite mistaken. We are not three opium smugglers. We are three gentlemen who wouldn't dream of touching opium."

Septimius then had a bright idea. He stepped forward, held out his dice to the inspector, and declared solemnly: "As sure as these dice will roll boxcars, we are three gentlemen."

Septimius confidently dropped the dice on the deck and everybody burst into guffaws. Three and one. It was a miracle. Septimius had not rolled boxcars.

The inspector told his men to load the three trunks onto the police launch and ordered Duncan and his friends to follow their baggage.

"You can continue on course undisturbed. I'll take these three gentlemen along with me. When you dock, please present yourselves as witnesses. Miss Bleecker, my profoundest apologies for the inconvenience."

Duncan, Septimius, and Clegg, handcuffed together, could see Kitty waving her handkerchief from the bridge of the *Jeannette*.

"Inspector," said Duncan, "may I say something?"

"Remember that anything you say can be held against you," the inspector warned in the admirable tradition of the American police.

"I know that," Duncan replied.

"Go ahead then."

"I would like you to take into account two important facts in this case. First, you've made a tragic error. Second, I would like you to free one of my hands. A man, even a gentleman, cannot perform the humble but necessary task of blowing his nose trussed up like a turkey."

"Thanks for the tip, but I'll blow your nose. Gentlemen like you get along better trussed up."

The inspector blew Duncan's nose, then had to blow Septimius's too. However, he was forced to uncuff Clegg. Clegg had asked too much.

The three gentlemen didn't get much more than a fleeting glimpse of the port of New York. It was already evening and there was a windowless wagon waiting to pick them up, rush them off, and unload them at the customs building.

Duncan, Clegg, and Septimius were dragged in front of a big desk presided over by a dignified magistrate.

"Good fishing today!" the inspector crowed.

"What did you catch?"

"Smugglers."

"What kind?"

The inspector was beside himself with glee. He and a policeman lifted Duncan's trunk and dropped it on the desk. Then he raised the lid, and, bowing, he said with the smugness of a trainer who has put a Bengal tiger through his paces, "*Voilà!*"

The magistrate peered into the trunk with some interest, then looked at the inspector. "Well now, this is the first time I've had to deal with a potato smuggler..."

"Potatoes?" the inspector said, squinting into the trunk.

"Unless I've been eating mashed opium with my lamb chops for forty years, those are potatoes in there," the magistrate pointed out.

The inspector approached Duncan. "Would you like to tell me," he growled, "how these potatoes made their way into this trunk, and where did the opium go?"

"You'd better ask the potatoes," said Duncan, impassive. "I wasn't inside the trunk."

The inspector clenched his fists but the magistrate stepped between them authoritatively. The inspector narrated what had happened aboard the *Jeannette* and insisted that the three had never touched the trunks.

"This is the work of some evil spirit!" he concluded.

"I'd say, on the other hand, it's the work of the other people who were on the boat," the magistrate objected. "It wouldn't have been too difficult to replace these trunks with another three prepared in advance."

The inspector was very perplexed.

It was useless for them to hope to be able to track down the *Jeannette*. It was nighttime and overcast. Anyhow, thinking back carefully, the inspector had to admit the *Jeannette*'s engines were a lot larger than a scow that size ordinarily needed. Who knew where the *Jeannette* was by now?

The inspector therefore turned all his fury on the three unfortunate prisoners. "All right, the comedy is over. But you'll pay for everything. Because tomorrow morning I'm not going to find three trunks full of potatoes, I'm going to find three opium smugglers."

Duncan bridled. "I hate to quibble, I know what a state you must be in, but I really must make two objections. One, if there's been a comedy, we weren't a part of it except insofar as everybody else has had a good laugh at our expense. Two, tomorrow morning you won't find three smugglers in a cell, only three gentlemen. I mentioned this fact before, as you will recall."

"If things are the way the inspector says they are," said Septimius, stretching out on a cot in the cell, "then Kitty is probably even better at practical jokes than Clotilda Troll. However, if I'm not mistaken, we're in a bit of a jam."

"Do you think they'll shoot us?" Clegg gurgled in terror.

"Not a chance," Duncan reassured him. "In the State of New York they don't have firing squads. They hang you instead."

"But we're gentlemen," whimpered Clegg.

"That's precisely why we have to worry," sighed Duncan.

9

The next morning the three gentlemen were once again dragged up before the magistrate. The inspector stood at his side.

"Are you prepared to reveal your true identities, which obviously have nothing to do with these passports, or would you rather be put through the third degree?"

"Beg your pardon for answering a question with a question," Duncan said. "Would it be possible, in the interest of justice, for you to talk to our Consul General, Lord Naderley? He'd be able to clear up this question of our identities immediately."

While a detective went off to the consulate, Duncan briefly recapitulated how he and his two companions (luckily landing on Bess in a dinghy after the yacht could not pull closer to shore) fell into the hands of a gang of outlaws.

"Mr. Troll, our countryman and friend," Duncan concluded, carefully avoiding any mention of Clotilda, "had lent us his villa on Bess Island. But somebody got there ahead of us."

The inspector laughed, very amused. "I never heard an alibi so simple and lily-white," he exclaimed, "in thirty years of dealing with gangsters."

"I'm sure I couldn't say," Duncan admitted, "but in

thirty years of dealing with gentlemen I've heard thousands."

An attendant notified them that the consul, Lord Naderley, was in the waiting room. That illustrious personage was ushered in immediately. As soon as he saw Duncan, he rushed over to embrace him. "Our own dear Duncan!" the consul exclaimed joyfully. "What a marvelous surprise! My heavens, here's Mr. Clegg too, and, if my eyes don't deceive me, Mr. North!"

Then he noticed the magistrate. "How do you do, Captain," the consul said. "What can I do for you?"

The magistrate explained that it was only a question of formalities: the identification of these three gentlemen who were arrested after a routine customs disturbance.

Duncan, Clegg, and Septimius were asked to go out to the waiting room for a moment while the magistrate explained the details. The consul started to laugh.

"Duncan, an opium smuggler? But, captain, Duncan Fitzmorris three weeks ago inherited two million pounds! Please, if I must, I shall have to ask my government to intervene."

The magistrate reassured the consul: he would have the three gentlemen released at once and convey to them the formal apologies of the government of the United States of America.

"My boat sails in an hour," the consul advised them, "so there's no point in your sending depositions over to the consulate. I'll take your word for it that you'll release them."

He embraced Duncan and was off.

The inspector was pale and dismayed, but the magistrate didn't lose his calm manner. He apologized to Duncan and the other two prisoners and asked them to be patient for a few more hours. "The American process of justice is unfortunately hampered by tedious bureaucratic necessities," he said ruefully.

But Duncan showed his generosity. Even if it took as long as a day, he didn't mind. "It's better this way," he said when they were back in their cell. "We'll have time to figure out what to do, since we won't have a farthing when we get out."

Clegg objected that the consul . . .

"The consul's already sailed," said Duncan. "Anyhow, a Fitzmorris never asks anybody for anything."

There was a moment of silence in the cell. Then Barton Clegg couldn't resist expressing his point of view. "And to think all it would take is a few drops of castor oil . . ."

Duncan wouldn't let him continue. "For three hundred years the Fitzmorrises and the Mayberrys were at each other's throats. Then there was a reconciliation, and my father, Tom Fitzmorris, married my mother, Jasmine Mayberry. No Fitzmorris will ever tip his hat to a Mayberry. Duncan Fitzmorris will never drink Jasmine Mayberry's castor oil!"

In the meantime the magistrate had come to some conclusions and was explaining his plan to the inspector.

"To release these three nuisances this soon will mean an end to our careers. We'll wind up back on the beat on the lookout for pickpockets and tarts on Broadway or at Barnum's Circus. The newspapers already know something and if we let them interview these three famous smugglers, we'll be on the spot. In no time at all we'll be the laughing stock of the entire country, with our three trunks of opium miraculously changed into three trunks of potatoes. Front page, I tell you. Tomorrow every hash house in the States will serve Smugglers' Potatoes and every dope pusher in the city will yell

There go the Potato Eaters! when we go by. The consul thinks everything's fine but he's gone, so we're safe till he gets back. We can't let those three out until we track down the real smugglers on the *Jeannette*. We have to take precautions. We're just two blind men groping around in the dark. The thing we must do is find an air-tight excuse to keep them locked up."

The inspector agreed. Then he asked, "What if they want out on bail?"

The magistrate shrugged. "They haven't got a dime and they can't get in touch with anybody. And besides, nobody knows they're here. The consul won't be back for a couple of months. Meanwhile we have enough time to bring in thousands of smugglers."

Two or three hours after this conversation, Duncan and his two companions found themselves in a real prison cell. Before the cell door was shut, Clegg asked the inspector, who'd brought them there, whether they could be let out on bail.

"Oh, sure," said the inspector, embarrassed. "But in this sort of case the bail is set very high. At the very least, ten grand. It's really not worth it," he hastened to add. "Better just be patient. Only a matter of hours, a day at the most."

A day passed. And another day. On the evening of the third day, Clegg sighed. "What with this infernal bureaucracy, we'll probably be here a week. It's not that bad, I guess, but it's tiresome. If only we had ten thousand dollars, we'd be out of here in fifteen minutes. What do you say, Mr. Fitzmorris?"

"Absolutely," Duncan said acidly. He was getting bored.

Clegg brought the subject up again the evening of the fourth day. "Sorry to bother you again, Mr. Fitzmorris, but you wouldn't know where to raise ten thousand dollars?"

"No, I wouldn't," Duncan snarled.

The fifth night Clegg let out another sigh. "It must be a very sad thing, to grow old in prison. Just think, Mr. Fitzmorris. If only you knew where to find ten thousand dollars. Isn't that so, Mr. North?"

"There's no point in going on like this, Mr. Clegg," Septimius said. "Evidently Mr. Fitzmorris enjoys being in jail. Otherwise . . ."

Duncan jumped to his feet: "Otherwise what?"

"Otherwise the most insignificant sacrifice on your part would bring you not ten thousand dollars but two million pounds."

Duncan felt the Fitzmorris rear up in him. "I'd rather stay in prison for a hundred years than drink that glass of castor oil!"

Duncan spent the sixth day on his bunk, while Clegg made poetic speeches about vegetable oils in general, with special emphasis on the merits of castor oil. "In Batik," Clegg commented around seven in the evening, "where castor oil is unknown, the average life span is only thirty-five years." Then he began on miscarriages of justice, which lasted for another two hours, about people left to languish in prison for twenty years, citing examples of men who had killed themselves beating their brains out on the cell walls. Toward midnight Duncan sat up and growled fiercely, "All right, how would you manage it? Here I am in America . . ."

Clegg and Septimius were pretending to be asleep but jumped down from their bunks and were instantly at Duncan's side. "Very simple. All you have to do is write your lawyer to come here right away with the castor oil."

"No! I'd rather die!" And he lay back on his bunk.

Duncan woke up late. He'd dreamed the entire first part of *The Count of Monte Cristo,* that is, the story of the Abbot Faria in the dungeon of the Château d'If, and it had been long and tedious. When he opened his eyes it was ten o'clock, and there, staring down at him, were Septimius and Clegg, respectively holding a pen and a bottle of ink, and a piece of paper with an envelope.

"I shot crap with the warder," Septimius explained. "I won six million dollars, the entire prison, and his wife. I settled for pen, ink, paper, and his promise to mail the letter."

Duncan laughed nastily. "Never! I said never, and a Fitzmorris always means what he says."

Around noon Duncan came out of his shell. "Anyhow, I'll bet that shoddy-looking pen won't write," he said with disdain. Then he dipped the point into the inkwell Septimius shakily held out and gracefully wrote at the head of the page, "New York, 7 June 1905."

"This is a nail, not a pen!" Duncan decided, throwing the pen down carefully so as not to damage the point.

At 4 p.m., after hovering over the pen and inkwell all afternoon whistling, Duncan took the pen in his hand casually, as if to doodle away the time. Then he wrote under the date, "Dear Mr. Dickson: Come to New York immediately and bring along the witnesses and the cast—"

Just then the warden brought in their afternoon bread.

Clegg broke open his loaf and discovered it contained a hammer and chisel. Septimius found a strong silk cord in his. The third loaf, intended for Duncan, contained a jasmine-scented note: *Darling Duncan, Loosen the bars of the window and climb down into the alley around eight o'clock. Everything's arranged for a riot in front of the prison. There will be a yellow cart waiting at the entrance to the alley. Get in and say, It's us three, let's go. I love you. Yours, Kitty.*

Duncan picked up the ink, pen, and paper and threw them out the window.

They had four hours left, and it wasn't going to be any problem to take out the bars in that time.

They wrapped some rags around the hammer and chisel to muffle the noise and Duncan began to chip cautiously. But the wall was harder than he'd expected. After a while he lost his temper and began pounding like a madman.

"Quiet in there!" came a voice from another cell. "There are those of us who'd like to sleep!"

Then the warder came in. "What, are you crazy?" he howled. "You want to get me fired? What kind of a way is that to hammer?"

"Let's see if you can do a better job," Duncan said nervously, handing him the hammer and chisel.

The warder tried it but made more noise than Duncan. "Look, I'm not supposed to hear a thing. If you keep this up, the warden at Sing Sing will hear it. I'll have to get you a saw or you'll never get anywhere," he said as he left the cell.

A few minutes later he was back with the saw. "Make sure you don't break it," he begged them. "It's my personal saw, not state property. When you see that blond dame, tell her for the loan of the saw it's another fifty bucks."

"Don't worry," Duncan reassured him as he set to work. Clegg wasn't any help in the operation because he was shaking too much. It was only thanks to the warder's lending a hand that the bars finally gave way at two minutes of eight.

It was the devil's own chore and more work than Duncan had ever done in his life. But they were free at last. Duncan heaved a sigh and set to knotting the cord around one of the stumps in the window ledge. Just then they heard footsteps and a voice shouted, "I'm at 195."

One ninety-five was the three companions' cell. The bars were feverishly replaced. Duncan managed it just in time. The door opened and an officer came in. "Follow behind me in single file."

Duncan, Septimius, and Clegg trudged crestfallen through the dark, damp corridors. So it was all over.

Another officer handed over the three men's documents and personal effects in the waiting room. "Sign here," he said, pointing to a sheet covered with tiny print. Duncan, Septimius, and Clegg signed.

"You're free for the time being," the officer told them, blotting their signatures. "Somebody posted bail for you."

Duncan was puzzled. "If you don't mind telling us," he asked, "who put up the money?"

"A lady name of Troll. She's outside waiting for you."

Duncan was a man of quick decisions. "Do you mind if we go back upstairs to pick up our handkerchiefs? We left them hanging out the window to dry."

"I'll send a warder up," the officer offered gallantly. Duncan smiled.

"I'd rather go, for sentimental reasons. I want to see the place where we suffered so much for the last time. You won't deny me that, will you?" The officer smiled.

Duncan headed off, took the stairs and corridors at a run, entered the cell, pulled down the bars, knotted the cord, let it drop, and swung himself to the pavement below, burning his hands on the rope. The alley was empty. The man Kitty sent must have misinterpreted the delay and fled after ten minutes of waiting. Duncan strolled down the alley. He was in the clear with the American law and his own pride.

Therefore it didn't shake him up when he heard footsteps behind him. And there was nothing to worry about anyway, because it was just Septimius and Clegg.

"Thanks, friends," Duncan exclaimed, squeezing their hands. "We're perfectly free now. Most important, free of Clotilda Troll."

They left the alley. In front of the gate to the prison there was an open carriage containing a distinguished-looking, obese gentleman.

Duncan approached him. "How do you do, George Ludens."

"Oh, my! Duncan Fitzmorris!" Georgie exclaimed.

"Would you be good enough to inform Miss Troll that we left by the servants' entrance so as to avoid the pleasure of seeing her pretty face?"

Georgie nodded to say yes and with his jaw hanging watched Duncan, Septimius, and Clegg disappear into the crowd.

The evening of June 7, 1905, was descending on the metropolis. The bluish flames of thousands upon thousands of gas lamps were lit one after another in houses, streets, and shops. The crowds wandered along the sidewalks before the rows of stores, a sea of heads sweeping past the displays. Between these twin streams of humanity, another river of omnibuses, streetcars, carriages, and wagons. Horses, thousands of them, the cracking of whips, the peal of bells.

Overhead, smoke, sparks, and the thunder of the El, the airborne railroad. Huge illuminated signs showing spacious rooms on wheels in which women in evening dress conversed, seated in silken armchairs, with elegant gentlemen.

Two rivers of people on both sides of every street, and out of the multitude sprang, tall and ungainly, the great Indians, the Napoleonic soldiers, the fat Dutchmen, the blackamoors of wood, who, huge pipes or cigars jutting from their mouths, guarded the entrances of all the tobacco shops. Swarms of boys hawking newspapers. From time to time, the deafening clatter of fire-wagon bells, the pressure-boiler emitting clouds of smoke. Wild galloping horses, the glint of copper helmets.

Every so often, a maelstrom in the stream: an eddy, a windmill of shouts, out of which some ragamuffin would scamper, or a man with a black eye, or a sobbing woman missing her pocketbook or shopping bags.

Twilight was falling on June 7 of 1905. Our three unhappy heroes were walking silently toward the howling mob.

"We're not exactly in a bed of roses now," Duncan noted after a while.

"If we had a guide, at least we could decide intelligently which bridge to spend the night under," Septimius complained.

"Ah freedom, blissful freedom," sighed Barton Clegg. But he hung his head like a student caught without his homework when Duncan and Septimius both shot him an evil look.

10

Mousquet narrates in his *Tales of the Old World* that M. Bertrand, finding himself the guest of Mme de Staël, confessed to having once spent the night on a park bench in the Bois de Boulogne. He ended his story with this observation: "There's no comparison between a marble bench and a feather bed." Even admitting that New World park benches, usually made of wood, are softer than those in the Bois de Boulogne, it isn't too difficult to understand how our three gentlemen, waking the following morning, could not help agreeing with M. Bertrand on the subject of park benches.

They dragged their aching bones and puffy eyes out of the park and entered New York. The tornado of people had already raised its ugly head. The coffee shops were overflowing with men and women devouring rolls and marmalade, ham and eggs. Septimius asked Duncan how long he thought a human being could survive without food.

"That depends," Duncan answered.

"I thought as much," Septimius said very thinly.

The three men walked a bit farther in silence. Then Clegg shook his head and stopped. "I can't go on," said Clegg. "My leg's out of joint."

Duncan and Septimius looked closely at Clegg's legs. Clegg's left foot had done a complete about-face, while his right was pointing in the proper direction. That is to say, while Clegg's right foot aimed forward, his left aimed straight backward.

"Are you in pain?" the two men asked in unison.

"No, it's just hard to walk. This always happens when I walk too much. My legs begin to disagree with each other, as it were. The right wants to keep moving ahead and the left wants to go home. Eventually everything gets back to normal."

Duncan approached a passer-by and then returned with the answer to his question. "Let's go," he said. "It's only a block away."

Clegg protested, but the two men held him up between them and forced him to walk.

They arrived at something that appeared to be a ticket window. Duncan rang the bell and asked for the manager. It was a matter of great urgency, he said.

They were led into a large room whose walls were lined with shelves. Although his face was covered with several days' beard, Duncan played the Fitzmorris to the hilt, very distinguished and gushing charming, elegant prose. When an austere-looking gentleman with a great handlebar mustache presented himself, Duncan's impeccable manners immediately enabled him to enlist the man's sympathy for Clegg's plight.

The estimable doctor—that was what Duncan dubbed him—had a close look at Clegg's leg, asked Clegg to walk around the room, and then wanted to know how and when this had begun. Afterwards he drew Duncan into an adjoining room.

Fifteen minutes later Duncan was back, radiating satisfaction. "Just a few more minutes while the doctor makes out the papers. I sold him on the idea."

Clegg's eyes opened wide and he asked Duncan what precisely it was that he'd been able to sell.

"Why, your leg, of course!" Duncan exclaimed. "He only wanted to buy the foot, but I made him understand that a foot without its leg is like a flower without a stem. He wouldn't give us any more than ninety dollars. But I've got another idea."

"You—you—" Clegg stammered, "you sold my leg? I won't allow it! Mr. Fitzmorris, that's immoral. A true gentleman does not sell his friend's leg!"

"A true gentleman never misses a chance to help his friends," Duncan pronounced severely. "A true gentleman is never selfish. A true gentleman would never starve himself or his friends out of petty pride. I evidently misjudged you, Mr. Clegg. Take back your leg. In the last analysis, of course you're right, the law does say that the leg belongs to you. Just as the law said Saint Martin's cloak belonged to Saint Martin, although Saint Martin did share it with his brother, the beggar who was freezing to death. Then again, Saint Martin was a gentleman . . ."

"Forgive me, Mr. Fitzmorris," Clegg stammered, blushing. "Forget every vulgar word that crossed my lips. You mustn't think ill of me. I am a gentleman just as Saint Martin was, and I will share my leg with my two hungry brothers."

"I'm very grateful to you," Duncan said, "and I'm sure Mr. North feels the same way."

Septimius bowed to Clegg and sat down again.

"Mr. Fitzmorris," Clegg whispered with tears in his eyes, "would you do me one favor: if anything happens to me during the operation . . ."

Duncan was stunned for a moment. Then he put his hands on Clegg's shoulders. "You must think they're going to cut off your leg! You're a far greater gentleman than Saint Martin, Mr. Clegg. A cloak doesn't begin to compare with a leg. But please don't worry. All you have to do is sign a paper willing your leg to Doctor Glinsky's hospital and it will be given to them on your death."

Clegg heaved a sigh of relief and Septimius wiped the sweat off his own forehead. The papers were signed, Clegg's leg was measured and catalogued, and finally the ninety dollars were handed over.

Poor Clegg had to walk around with them all day long. But at dusk Duncan totaled it up and said they now had $820. The leg had been bought by eight other clinics.

"Doesn't it seem to you, Mr. Fitzmorris, as if this whole deal is a little irregular?" Clegg asked timidly.

"Not in the slightest, Mr. Clegg. There may be nine beneficiaries, but they all have science in common and science is unique. The important thing is to study the phenomenon for the progress of science."

"Admirable!" Septimius agreed.

"Fine," said Clegg. "The only problem is, although it's a perfect imitation, my leg is made of wood covered with rubber."

Eight hundred twenty dollars in the hands of three men does not go a long way. Especially if the three men have to buy new wardrobes and take a suite in a good hotel.

Septimius was the one to sound the alarm after a couple of weeks: they had to find a source of income immediately.

Luckily Clegg soon came across an ad in the *New York Herald:* WANTED: GENTLEMEN. URGENT!

The three gentlemen hurried over to the address given and found themselves in a waiting room full of people. Men, women, children, waitresses, Negroes, gaudily dressed ladies. Duncan, Septimius, and Clegg were led into a smoky room partially filled by an enormous man wedged into an armchair, smoking a cigar and wearing a hat.

"Are you the fellow who's advertising for gentlemen?" asked Duncan as the fat man hung up the phone.

"Yeah, that's right. Where are they?"

"We are they," Duncan explained.

The fat man began to giggle. "You, gentlemen? Are you kidding me? I send the likes of you over to Mrs. Thompson's place and it's the end of a nice relationship."

This didn't upset Duncan. "I hate to disillusion you, sir, but we really are gentlemen. We even have the papers to prove it."

The fat man looked through their credentials. "In that case," he said after a while, "since you're foreigners, well, with foreigners anything goes. But just so you know where I stand, I don't buy it. Peggy!" he shouted.

A good-looking redhead appeared. "Peggy," the fat man said, "get a load of these foreigners who claim to be gentlemen. What do you think, we can send them over to Mrs. Thompson's?"

Peggy loftily eyed Duncan, Septimius, and Clegg. She made a gesture that meant stand up straight. Then she shrugged. "Well, it's a night reception," she whispered. "If they stay out of the light they might do."

Duncan smiled. "At home we're thought of as perfect gentlemen even in broad daylight. Let me assure you, miss, we won't make you ashamed of us."

"Do you have penguin suits?" the fat man inquired.

"If you mean evening clothes, yes."

"All right, two dollars a night. When I provide the penguin suits, it's only one-fifty. In any case, watch yourselves!"

"In what sense?" Duncan asked.

"In the sense that, number one, if so much as a spoon is missing, your face gets smashed in. Number two, no picking up cigar butts. Three, no booze. Four, only two trips through the buffet line. Five, no swiping pastries and stuffing them into your pockets. Six, no swearing, spitting on walls or ceiling. Seven, no slapping guests on the back. Eight, don't speak unless you're spoken to. Mrs. Thompson will tell you what to say in case somebody does talk to you. In case you break any of the rules, you'll never see that two dollars."

Peggy put in a word. "Above all, no passes at any of the ladies."

Duncan spread his arms helplessly. "We can go along with one through eight, but about number nine, well, it depends."

"Depends on what?"

"If I found myself face to face with a girl as beautiful as you are, it wouldn't be a question of two dollars, it would be losing two thousand."

The fat man pushed his hat back. "Look here, punk," he growled, "how would you like to lose a mouthful of teeth?"

Duncan bowed. "If I weren't sure I could flatten you with one blow to the jaw, and if I weren't convinced you're a man of the world with a sense of humor, I would never have permitted myself to compliment this lady in your presence."

The fat man visually measured Duncan's shoulders and then smiled. "Can't imagine why I thought different, plain as the nose on your face you're a gentleman."

Then taking stock of Septimius's shoulders, which were if anything more impressive than Duncan's, he added, "That includes you."

Clegg's shoulders, however, were not so imposing.

The fat man eyed him with disdain. Peggy intervened. "Can you dance?"

"Very well," answered Duncan, smiling.

"Good, good," the fat man exclaimed. "Three dollars a night for dancing with any lady the hostess asks you to. Also you get four trips to the buffet. Only punch to drink, though. Mrs. Thompson complained about the last two gentlemen I sent her because you could smell the breath on them all the way across the room. No booze! And hands off the necklaces! You have such business, take it some place else, not to Mrs. Thompson's."

"Agreed," Duncan said.

"Okay, it's a deal. Here's a buck in advance. At nine tonight you come by here. I want to check to see you look all right."

At nine o'clock Duncan, Septimius, and Clegg presented themselves to the fat man in impeccable evening dress.

"I'm fainting," he said. "Just like real gentlemen. Look here, you, are you up to playing a count?"

"Why not?" said Duncan. "I *am* a count."

The fat man shook his head, but Peggy was looking at Duncan languidly.

"Fine, you play the count the way a count's supposed to be, I'll give you five bills instead of three. You only speak English?"

"No, I speak French, Spanish, Italian, German, and Russian as well."

The fat man pounded his fists on the table with glee. "A regular gold mine! Russian counts sell like hotcakes here. Mrs. Thompson shells out seven smackers for a Russian count."

Duncan, Septimius, and Clegg bowed so impressively that the fat man didn't know what to make of it. Then he blushed, took off his hat, and bowed back awkwardly. Peggy sighed. Then the three gentlemen departed.

"That one," the fat man commented, "either he's an international jewel thief or he's a count for real."

At Mrs. Thompson's home Duncan and the two other gentlemen stood in the foyer while the butler kept an eye on them. After an interminable wait, Mrs. Thompson turned up.

"Now let's have a look at you three," Mrs. Thompson said with authority. She turned on the lights and stood back to get the overall impression. On first inspection they seemed satisfactory. "Thank goodness, at least you're well dressed. The last fellow your boss sent had holes in his socks. Now walk around."

Duncan and his two companions paraded uncomfortably around the room.

"You're about as graceful as cowboys," Mrs. Thompson commented after she'd watched them through her lorgnette. "But, as I said, nice-looking clothes. I do like those clothes. Your boss should always dress his people in clothes like these. Do walk as little as possible," she admonished them. "I'll tell you when to walk."

"Yes, ma'am," said Duncan, bowing.

"And bear in mind there are two private detectives stationed in the ballroom," she warned them severely. "Keep your hands where they belong. I definitely do like those clothes. Really first-rate. Have you got weapons in your pockets?"

Duncan, Septimius, and Clegg turned out their pockets for her benefit.

"All right," Mrs. Thompson approved, still ogling their clothes. Then something crossed her mind. "And the count? Where's this count your boss promised me?"

Duncan bowed. "I am the count."

Mrs. Thompson gestured impatiently. Then, after she'd studied Duncan more closely through the lorgnette, she seemed reassured. "But . . ." she paused. "Precisely what kind of count do you intend playing?"

"The man at the agency said you'd prefer a Russian count," Duncan explained. But Mrs. Thompson shook her head violently.

"I don't want any part of Russian counts," she said emphatically. "Everybody's got a Russian count now. None of this Russian count business. Even the middle class has Russian counts at their functions. Can't you be another nationality?"

"I could play an English lord, a German baron, a French count, an Italian prince . . ."

"Right, let's try the French count, nobody has one yet. Yes, absolutely, a French count. Let's see you do the French count."

Duncan stood still. Mrs. Thompson lost her temper. "Come on, young man! Where's this French count act? Don't stand there like a stick!"

Duncan smiled. "Really, Mrs. Thompson, French counts who don't have anything to do can only stand precisely the way I am standing. A French count must have occasion to show that he is a French count. Standing still, one count looks much the same as a count of any other nationality."

Mrs. Thompson had to agree that Duncan had a point.

"Let's see," she said after a little thought. "French counts are something special. I remember one night over at Mrs. Voght's there was a French count who made a big hit singing *Volga Volga*. Then he did a marvelous dance, squatting with his arms crossed. He was perfectly charming."

"Madam," Duncan began, "if I may be so bold, usually it's Russian counts who sing *Volga Volga* and do that sort of dance. But I must say, never in public. He must have been a counterfeit Russian count."

"Yes, yes," Mrs. Thompson exclaimed. "Of course, everybody knows that. Never mind. I can't remember for the life of me what a French count does. *Think,* young man. What are you going to do?"

"If you don't mind," Clegg interrupted, "I'd like to suggest that the central characteristic of a French count is gallantry. Better than anybody else, a French count knows how to compliment a lady."

"Finally. There we have it!" Mrs. Thompson exclaimed. "Of course: gallantry, chivalry, poetry, Latin blood, romanticism, everything romantic. A French count who isn't romantic isn't worth his salt."

Mrs. Thompson sat down on a sofa and told Clegg and Septimius to move to the other side of the room. Then she invited Duncan to sit beside her.

"All right, young man. Show me how a French count makes a compliment."

Duncan straightened his cravat, coughed lightly, and began to speak in a soft voice. "Madam," he said, "I love you."

"Oh, for heaven's sake!" Mrs. Thompson exclaimed. "Don't be so trite."

Duncan didn't bat an eyelash and continued in an even sweeter voice. "Yes, madam, it is trite. Everything of any importance in life is trite. Birth—death—everyone's born, everyone dies, everyone falls in love. It may be banal to tell an ordinary woman one loves her, but it is not banal to be in love with you. On the contrary. It is the most original thing in the world because you are the most beautiful woman in the world. To admire a flower is tedious, but to admire the most beautiful flower in all America is ecstasy. I do love you, madam, and I want to kiss your delicious lips, I want to caress your soft hair . . ." Duncan went on diligently to list all the things he wanted to do to the exquisite Mrs. Thompson as his voice became tenderer, sweeter, more seductive.

After a while Mrs. Thompson threw her arms around him and sighed, "My darling . . ."

Septimius and Clegg, watching from the other side of the room, couldn't restrain their enthusiasm. They exploded into bravos.

Mrs. Thompson started, tore away from Duncan, and jumped to her feet. "Fine. Admirable. Perfect," she stammered as she pulled herself together. "Very well done. But tone it down a little. I don't need any scandals. You know what I mean, Count?"

The grand ballroom of the Thompsons' house was beautifully decorated that evening and mobbed with important people and ladies covered with jewelry. Clegg and Septimius behaved very well and made a good impression on everybody. But Duncan absolutely shone. He was earning his seven dollars in spades: he made hundreds of compliments, danced with every woman in the room including the decrepit ones, and executed a myriad of stunning bows.

The champagne and foul mixed drinks that Americans serve at parties lent a certain gaiety to the reception, but Duncan grew more bored by the minute. To keep himself awake, he decided to woo the wife of a banker named Babbitt. A quarter of an hour later, the estimable lady promised to start divorce proceedings against Babbitt the next day. Duncan excused himself delicately and withdrew to the terrace. Twenty minutes later a Mrs. Mayfair was whispering into his ear that the crowd and their boisterousness were depressing her and why didn't the two of them . . .

Yes, things were getting monotonous. Duncan hurried back into the ballroom. There his boredom disappeared. Mrs. Thompson introduced Duncan to the magnificent Spanish countess Mercedes de la Sierra, and he had the honor of accompanying her out to the terrace for a breath of fresh air, since the heavy atmosphere in the ballroom had got a bit on the distinguished lady's nerves.

"Kitty, what on earth are you doing here?" Duncan asked the beautiful blonde once they were alone.

"Duncan," the blonde sobbed, "how could you have done that to me? Why didn't you come down at eight? That idiot driver ran off when you were taking so long. He was terrified."

"I managed on foot," Duncan explained. "I repeat, what are you doing here?"

"Duncan, dear Duncan," Kitty answered. "Obviously I'm playing the Spanish countess."

"Don't tell me you were sent by the agency too?" Duncan recounted the story of their employment, which much amused Kitty. Then she explained she was working on a man she had met the night before.

"Opium?"

"No."

"A swindle?"

"No," said Kitty. "Marriage."

"In that case, it's serious," said Duncan. Then he escorted Kitty into the ballroom, because between one kiss and another she'd informed him that her beau was about to arrive.

Duncan and Kitty dived into the tempestuous waves of people and danced until Kitty exclaimed, "Look, Duncan, over there in the corner. He's talking to Mrs. Thompson."

Duncan glanced toward the corner of the room. Beside Mrs. Thompson was a corpulent, distinguished-looking gentleman with a girl in black on his arm.

"Duncan, that's him!" Kitty said proudly.

The dance was over and Kitty took Duncan by the arm. "Come on, I'll introduce you. You dance with the girl and give me a chance to work on him. Don't worry, he told me he was coming with his cousin. Be good now."

When the corpulent gentleman saw Kitty in front of him his eyes opened wide and the scene that followed was swift and dramatic.

CORPULENT GENTLEMAN (*embarrassed*): Why Countess, what a pleasant surprise . . . Let me introduce you to Miss Clotilda Troll . . . Clotilda, this is Countess de la Sierra, the one I told you about . . .

KITTY (*with surprise*): How do you do, Miss Troll.

CORPULENT GENTLEMAN (*breathlessly*): Clo, if you'll excuse me, Duncan, if I may . . . Countess, would you care to dance?

KITTY: Yes, yes, do let's dance, Mr. Ludens.

Kitty and Georgie disappeared in the mob of dancers and Duncan found himself face to face with Clotilda Troll.

11

Having landed on Bess while the *Jeannette* was shrinking in the distance, Clotilda and her fiancé Georgie had found the villa in a shambles and not a trace of Duncan, Septimius, or Clegg. Except this message pinned to the door, which explained everything: *Prisoners of band of opium smugglers commanded by lady named Kitty and man named Bill. Left on board* Jeannette. *10 a.m. 29 May 1905. Barton Clegg.*

"That must be the boat we spotted as we were coming in!" Clotilda exclaimed, wild-eyed. "Georgie, we absolutely must track down those smugglers!"

"Well, really," Georgie stammered. He thought the best idea was to keep as far away from the smugglers as possible.

But she didn't let him say it. "Georgie! Board the ship!"

The captain was given permission to let the boilers blow up if necessary, but they had to catch up with the *Jeannette*, which was now barely a spot on the horizon. Clotilda said nothing during the furious chase. Every plank and joint in the *Dolphin* groaned, and the sweat-drenched stokers eyed the gauges with terror. The *Dolphin* flew over the water, but they never would have caught up with the *Jeannette* if it hadn't been for the customs patrol boat. It stalled the *Jeannette* for a good twenty minutes and the *Dolphin*—forgive the un-nautical terminology—was able to gain a lot of ground.

The distance between them was narrowed considerably and the *Dolphin* and *Jeannette* touched ground at almost precisely the same moment. Then finally Clotilda spoke, her voice trembling: "Georgie, if you love me, you'll go aboard that boat and free Duncan. Here's a gun. If necessary, shoot!"

Georgie muttered something and then went aboard the *Jeannette*. He went escorted by the entire crew of the *Dolphin,* all of whom were armed to the teeth and fully prepared to earn the two sizable banknotes Georgie had held up to them. The port where the *Jeannette* had docked was not New York. In fact, it wasn't even what one could call a port, just an inlet singularly lacking in harbor police and customs patrols. Georgie boarded the *Jeannette* and was immediately confronted by twenty men, each with his right hand tucked into his jacket pocket. This didn't please Georgie, but he didn't let himself lose heart.

"I'd like to speak with the captain," said Georgie, and Bill took a step forward. "I'd be very grateful for some news about three gentlemen who, we have reason to believe, are aboard your yacht," Georgie explained, smiling; but Bill didn't know a thing. What the devil three men could he be talking about?

"We never heard of no three gents," Bill said ungraciously. "This isn't a ferryboat. This is the pleasure yacht of Countess de la Sierra and we're here to take the countess wherever she feels like going."

"You have no idea where to find these three gentlemen?" Georgie pursued.

"If your friends are mixed up with opium, Feds, and so on, I'd suggest you go check out the New York City can," Bill said encouragingly.

Then Kitty came on deck. Georgie bowed.

"Captain, has something happened?" Kitty asked.

Bill winked at Georgie and then spat. "No, Countess," he said, "the man owns the yacht anchored alongside and came aboard to ask for directions. Their compass is on the blink."

"That's right, Countess, our compass is out of order," Georgie agreed. "On the blink, as he says. It's a nuisance, having your compass out of order, you know. You have to stop at every inlet to ask for directions."

That's how it happened. That was how Georgie met Countess de la Sierra, and although he knew perfectly well the so-called countess was in reality the Kitty of Clegg's note, he felt a very pleasant sensation creeping over him. They chatted for a few minutes.

"You're a very interesting man," Kitty decided. "I'd be delighted if we could meet next Wednesday, say at the Grand Mog about 5 p.m.?"

"So?" said Clo anxiously when Georgie reappeared.

"Everything's fine," Georgie said happily. "We might meet each other at the Grand Mog next Wednesday. Never met a more charming girl."

Clotilda was stunned for a moment, then asked who the charming girl was.

"The countess," Georgie explained.

"What countess?"

"The smuggler."

Clotilda grabbed Georgie's cravat. "*Where is Duncan?*" she shrieked.

"Duncan? Oh, Duncan. Don't worry, Clo, he's safe. He's in jail."

The *Dolphin* set off under full steam for New York. Clotilda calmed down after Georgie had told her everything. She even brightened up, on two counts: one, Duncan was no longer in danger and it was better to be in jail than among smugglers; and two, it was obvious that Georgie was falling in love.

There was one drawback. "You know I'm happy to see you falling in love with another woman, but did she have to be a smuggler?"

Georgie gave this some thought and then said, "When you think about it, Clo, it's likely that everything that's said or written about smugglers is speculation. The truth is different."

"Believe what you want," Clo said, shaking her head. "Nevertheless, to fall in love with a smuggler . . ."

Georgie put his arm around her. "Clotilda, I don't mean to be rude, but that fellow you're in love with is a smuggler too. Look at it this way. Wasn't he arrested for smuggling? You're worse off than I am, if anything. Duncan's in jail and Kitty isn't."

Clotilda held her breath. The impossible had occurred. Georgie was rebelling and throwing off the yoke. "I do hope you won't leave me all alone in this mess," she said finally. Her voice was very sad.

But Georgie's ears were still full of the gorgeous smuggler's voice and in no condition to catch innuendoes. "Clo," said Georgie, "I'm at your service until half past four Wednesday afternoon—no, make it four o'clock because I've got to go to the barber. After that, I don't know whether you'd better count on me. It depends..."

In New York Clotilda made good use of Georgie's last hours. They scattered a sackful of dollar bills throughout the portion of the police force patrolling the waterfront and finally discovered where Duncan and his companions had been locked up. They retained Smithson, the best lawyer in New York, who was able to spring the three men by posting $5,000 worth of bail.

Finally in the early evening of June 7, 1905, Clotilda dragged Georgie off to the prison and wasted a good thirty minutes waiting for Duncan to appear.

Eventually an officer came out and stretched out his arms desolately. "They escaped through the cell window," he said.

Georgie notified their consulate about Duncan, and Clotilda had to return to the hotel in a very frustrated state of mind.

With things as they were, how, one might object, could both Clotilda and Duncan find themselves at Mrs. Thompson's ball?

Don't you believe in Fate?

Yes, it was Fate. But Fate solely, exclusively in the guise of Clotilda Troll.

Five days went by following that eventful night at the prison. Clotilda set every detective agency in New York on Duncan's trail. He and the other two gentlemen had disappeared into the great canyons of the metropolis like three needles into a haystack. But Clotilda was far from losing hope. In fact Clotilda confidently bided her time.

Sure enough, on the morning of June 18, while Clo was listening to Georgie's inventory of the many exceptional qualities of Countess de la Sierra (now that he was in love with her, it kept slipping Georgie's mind that Clotilda considered the gorgeous blonde no better than a common smuggler, which she was), the maid announced that they had a visitor.

Shortly thereafter Barton Clegg was shown in. "It's taken me three days to find out where you were staying," Clegg said. "Thank heavens I've finally tracked you down."

Clotilda was amazed. "How did you know I was in New York?"

"I saw you on the *Dolphin* from the *Jeannette*. Did you find the note I left you? I was sure you would. Also I ran across the *Dolphin* down at the docks."

"Well done, Mr. Clegg!" Clotilda exclaimed, applauding. "I'll double your salary."

In certain situations, Georgie made a habit of sitting still and keeping his mouth shut. This was one of those situations. But at Clotilda's exclamation, he could contain himself no longer. "Sorry, Clo, I didn't catch the bit about the salary."

"Oh, poor Georgie," Clotilda said, giggling. "I never told you Clegg is our spy in the enemy camp. What would have been the point of playing this trick on Duncan without knowing his reactions to it?"

What Clotilda didn't explain was that she'd thrown Clegg in to protect Duncan. Instead she asked Clegg to tell her the whole story. So Clegg began.

"Once we got to Bess Island," Clegg said, "we fell into the hands of twenty evil ruffians, commanded by a lady named Kitty . . ."

Georgie suddenly interrupted. "Excuse me, Mr. Clegg, sorry, Clo, but I've got to run, and besides, it's not polite to eavesdrop on things that don't concern one."

It was a miracle Clotilda didn't laugh in Georgie's face.

"—a lady named Kitty," Clegg continued after Georgie left, "who luckily fell in love with Mr. Fitzmorris . . ."

Clotilda jumped. "Fell in love?" she asked impatiently. "What do you mean, fell in love?"

"I'd rather not go into the details," Clegg begged, blushing.

"Then please don't dwell on anything concerning that wretched woman!" Clotilda exploded. "Go on!"

Clegg laboriously told the whole story, and Clotilda asked with studied indifference. "After all this, what does Mr. Fitzmorris think of me?"

Clegg imploringly spread his arms. "It would seem as if his most ardent desire is never to set eyes on you or hear your name mentioned again."

"He doesn't hate me?"

"I wouldn't say so. Mr. Fitzmorris is an unusual man, Miss Troll. He made a few comments the first day and never spoke about you again."

Clotilda was undone. That simpleton was still going to be capable of greeting her with absolute indifference whenever they met, as if nothing had happened. For Clo, this was insupportable.

"When's he going back to New Islip?" she asked, her heart beating fast.

"It's hard to say," said Clegg. "Mr. Fitzmorris hasn't a farthing, and there's this problem of the opium-smuggling incident."

Clotilda started giggling. "What *are* you talking about? Mr. Fitzmorris inherited several million pounds only a month ago."

"He did not inherit and does not seem to intend to inherit the money. It's that business about the castor oil."

"Castor oil?"

Clegg recounted in great detail the story of the glass of castor oil. At the end of it, Clotilda leaped to her feet and let out a whoop of triumph.

"All is not lost! This changes things quite a bit. Do keep me informed of all developments. I must know everything!"

12

"Would it be indiscreet to ask you how you are, Mr. Fitzmorris?" said Clotilda, smiling.

"Not a bit, Miss Troll," Duncan replied, trying to act calmer than he really was. "I'm flattered by your interest in my health. I'm quite well, Miss Troll, and I hope you are too."

The duel was on. It wasn't going to be easy, but Clotilda was determined not to give an inch.

"I was most irritated by the disgraceful bureaucratic incompetence which allowed us to miss each other a few nights ago. I was anxious to learn whether your cruise had been pleasant."

"Very pleasant, Miss Troll. I can't tell you how much I enjoyed the fresh air on Bess. Delightful sojourn, I must say."

Clotilda recalled the details Clegg omitted to tell her, but she still didn't lose her elegant subtleness. "I can imagine, Mr. Fitzmorris, that your visit there was pleasurable. How could it have been otherwise, when you found yourself in such interesting company?"

Duncan sensed an irregularity in his nervous system. It was peculiar and disturbing. He therefore decided on tactical retreat. He smiled his famous half smile and excused himself. "I'm heartbroken, Miss Troll, but a previous engagement compels me to take leave of you, pleasant though your presence is. Good evening, Miss Troll."

Clotilda, with a similar smirk, gave him warning. "You'd best not, Mr. Fitzmorris. Otherwise you won't be paid that seven dollars for your services as a gentleman. My good friend Mrs. Thompson is very pleased with you, but she is nevertheless American and a very sharp businesswoman. I suggest you dance with me instead. It's in the contract, isn't it?"

Duncan waltzed Clotilda around the room with the same care he might have taken with an activated torpedo, not a beautiful millionairess.

Clegg and Septimius watched the eccentric couple with eyes wide as saucers.

"Frankly, I think he's going to break her neck," Septimius murmured.

"Mr. Fitzmorris is an exceptional person and would never give the slightest sign that he's aggravated," Clegg declared. But the two of them stood poised to run to Clo's rescue if necessary. There was no need.

Duncan maintained his remarkable calm, taking every precaution not to alter his dignified reserve.

"Seven dollars ought to provide one with a French count who's a bit livelier," Clotilda noted after a while.

Duncan stared at the chandelier.

"I'm sure Mrs. Thompson wouldn't have lied about you," Clotilda persisted. "I've got a French count for tonight who cost me only seven dollars but he's worth at least fifteen, she said. He knows the most delightful stories and he's so perceptive and seductive, that's what Mrs. Thompson said, and I believe her, she's a very dear friend. So why don't you tell me a delightful story or be perceptively seductive?"

Duncan smiled at Kitty, who was dancing cheek to cheek with Georgie.

It was a shabby trick. Duncan could feel himself losing ground. He would have strangled that idiot girl with glee. In fact, he was about to break down.

"You're just not cooperative," Clo sighed. "It isn't even important to you that we're from the same country, in fact the same city. That's the worst part of it, you're unpatriotic."

The dance was over. Duncan bowed and executed a perfect about-face. But Clotilda stopped him.

"Could it be that you're afraid to escort me out on the terrace, that you might thereby break the heart of a blond countess dancing in the vicinity?" Clotilda insinuated, feeling herself at last the mistress of a most trying situation.

Duncan, on the other hand, was lost. Yet he tried to reflect on the indomitable courage of birds on the wing and clenched his teeth. "Nothing in the world could induce me to decline the pleasure of being alone with you under the American stars."

It was a magnificent June night, a 1905 night with no noise of automobile horns to jar the stillness nor neon signs advertising the virtues of liquid shoepolish to blot out the starlit sky. Thousands and thousands of lights, but little ones, tiny azure gas flames. Strains of music, very Old World. The stars' reflection shimmered on the ocean and the deep lowing of some lost ship's foghorn sounded like the sigh of an enamored island.

The terrace was broad and filled with flowers and inviting shadows. Duncan leaned against the balustrade and stared out at the distant sea. Clotilda watched the sea in the distance too but her attention was on the nearby Duncan. Her voice was low and subdued. A girl confiding. "Duncan, do you forgive me?"

Duncan didn't move.

"Mr. Fitzmorris," Clotilda whispered, "the joke got out of hand. I didn't want you to get mixed up in anything as unpleasant as this. Mr. Fitzmorris, the truth is, I'm in love with you . . ."

"Not you too," Duncan said with great boredom. "Good lord, what frightful monotony, from smugglers to heiresses, women are all alike."

Duncan had more than won.

Their brief moment was destroyed.

Clotilda bit her lip. "I hate you!" she said through her teeth.

"You too?" Duncan said, yawning. "My, my, women are tedious."

Clotilda ran back into the ballroom. Septimius and Clegg were standing by the glass doors prepared to come running when Clotilda screamed, but after she had flown through the ballroom alone, they looked at each other in amazement.

"Evidently she was able to kill him," Septimius commented.

"Thank heavens," Clegg sighed. "If one of them had to go, I'm glad Miss Troll wasn't the corpse."

Then the corpse sauntered in from the terrace smiling and the mystery-to-be was cleared up at once. When Duncan finished his story, Septimius seemed very worried. "If she pulled this trick on you when she was in love with you, what's she going to do now that she hates you?"

Georgie barely had time to say goodbye to his countess. Clotilda had grabbed him by the arm and told him in a tone that admitted of no contradiction to take her back to their hotel.

"Georgie!" Clotilda howled once they were in the

carriage. "He would despise me even if I were the last woman on earth! Do you understand, Georgie?"

"I understand, yes," Georgie answered. "But in the last analysis the trick you pulled on him wasn't particularly conducive to love."

"What trick? What's that got to do with this?" she screamed. "I told him I loved him and do you know what that moron said to me? *Not you too!*"

"Duncan said that to you? Just like that?"

"Exactly that way."

"He really is exceptional," Georgie said, full of admiration. "That's a classic."

Clotilda declared she would throttle Georgie if he didn't stop passing comments of that nature. Georgie shut up.

"It's clear I'm going to have to kill that arrogant cretin," Clotilda shrieked.

"I think perhaps instead of killing him you ought to marry him," Georgie observed cautiously. "That would be a far worse punishment for him."

Clotilda at first thought she would murder Georgie on the spot, but then she decided not to. Maybe Georgie was right after all. She couldn't sleep and spent the whole night thinking. Perhaps too much.

13

The following day was very trying for our three gentlemen.

The fat man at the agency, on being confronted toward noon by Duncan, Septimius, and Clegg, could not restrain his enthusiasm. Mrs. Thompson had called to say how exceedingly pleased she'd been with their performance and that she was going to pay them double. She'd been particularly impressed with Duncan and was prepared to offer him a two-year contract at fifteen hundred dollars a week.

"Only problem is, Mrs. Thompson is very impulsive and ten to one she winds up marrying you," concluded the fat man. "But it *is* a job."

Duncan shook his head and said he didn't want to play the count role any more. He wanted to change his tack.

"In the long run, you're right," the fat man admitted. "Somebody on the ball like you shouldn't take the first job that comes along. Could do yourself out of at least another five hundred smackers. I'm not going to have any trouble finding work for you. Today, for instance, I might have a couple of interesting things."

The fat man asked if they'd mind working separately.

"Not at all," Duncan said.

"Great," said the fat man happily. "First let's make

out Clegg's schedule. There's a mass meeting this afternoon at the Cooper Institute. The bus drivers' union is staging a protest, they want goodness knows what benefits. Management asked me for a counterprotester. The bus drivers have six spokesmen but the important one is a fellow name of Bettel. He's the only one knows how to make a speech, but it's no sweat to throw him off. All he does is toss around big ideas and make loud noises for hours on end. Nothing to it. Just get him off the subject. Then he blows up and starts cussing. Next thing you know, the cops pick him up for disturbing the peace and that's the end of the protest. What do you say?"

"But . . . but . . ." Clegg stammered.

The fat man interrupted him. "It's not dangerous, if that's what you're thinking. These mass meetings work like so. In the auditorium you have management and six labor leaders. The bus drivers have to stay outside. In this case, you also have a bunch of cops and the company directors, that is, everybody fed up with bus drivers. As I said, bus drivers outside, making big noises at each other."

"All right, if that's the way it will be, I'll take the job," said Clegg, reassured.

"If you can make the audience laugh, you get fifteen bucks," the fat man explained. "They start booing and you have to shut up, it's only eight. They kick you out and I won't give you any more than four. You read?"

"Of course," Clegg said.

The fat man handed him a pamphlet. "The details are in here. Bettel's usual gripes are all written up. Read it and make sure you know what's going on. There's a seat reserved for you. Here's the ticket."

Clegg took the pamphlet and the ticket and the fat man went on. "Now here's a twenty-five-dollar divorce case. It involves arranging for the husband to catch you with the wife."

"I'll take it," said Septimius. "That's not bad, for twenty-five dollars."

The fat man laughed. "Don't I know it! But look here, I'm not giving away money. The twenty-five bills is on account of it's not quite so simple-minded."

"How's that? The lady isn't willing?" asked Septimius.

"Sure the lady's willing. The husband isn't. Also, he's a big brute with fists like so."

Septimius's shoulders were a yard wide and the fat man's gesture made him laugh.

"Here's your instruction sheets," the fat man told him. "In that closet there's some boxing gloves and a sandbag to take back to your hotel. Never hurts to practice. The lady says the trick's to punch him in the ribs, on account of his head is hard as rock."

Clegg and Septimius went out. "See you at the hotel tonight," said Duncan.

When they were alone the fat man rubbed his hands together. "I'm glad your friends are so easy to get along with," he said. "I've got something here fits you to a T. It's a five-hundred-dollar job for a lot of talent. You pull it off, you get a bonus."

Duncan nodded.

"You got to put one over on a guy and get him to do something."

"Let's get one thing straight: I'm no stool pigeon," Duncan said emphatically.

"Who said anything about stool pigeons! Stool pigions don't get but a fin a night. We're talking about half a grand here. For being a gentleman. All expenses paid. Besides that, you're no pigeon, you know more about these things than I do. Before you leap, do me the favor to look. Go over to the Imperial Hotel and ask for Mr. Striker."

Peggy, the good-looking redhead, had just come in. Duncan bowed.

"Now if you had asked me to visit this lovely creature instead of some idiot named Striker, things would be much more interesting," Duncan sighed.

Peggy smiled. The fat man took off his hat and hurled it at the wall.

"It's unjust," the fat man whimpered. "I get you a job fit for a millionaire, I make you a career, and you try to steal Peggy away from me!"

Duncan started to laugh. "Remember I'm a gentleman," he exclaimed. "There are certain things it's not proper for a gentleman to do. If I say Peggy's the best-looking girl on Broadway, I say it in all good faith, not to take Peggy away from you but because she's truly a splendid creature."

It was a long hard day for our three gentlemen.

Clegg, after reading his pamphlet on the bus situation, went off to the meeting and took a seat. Several imbeciles dressed in their Sunday clothes got up and babbled for a while. Then Bettel began a fiery speech on the organization of modern society and made some farfetched historical allusions.

All of a sudden Clegg stood up and demanded the floor. Then he made a light objection, just to test the wind. Bettel turned beet red and paused with visible annoyance. But he ceded the floor to Clegg. Immediately the man on Clegg's left began whispering in his ear: "I'll give you fifty bucks to get out of here."

The man on Clegg's right overheard and took up the opposition: "A hundred bucks if you stay and protest."

"One-fifty," the man on Clegg's left whispered.

"Two hundred," the man on his right answered.

"Two-fifty."

"Three hundred!"

"Three-fifty!"

"Four hundred!"

Clegg was stunned, caught in this auction. The two redfaced bidders made offer after offer through clenched teeth. Clegg's head was jerking back and forth like a chicken's.

"Twenty-six grand!" the man on the left said, finally.

"Twenty—" the man on the right began. Then he stopped. Applause and cheers filled the vaulting of the great hall and echoed out onto the street. Bettel had finished his declamation and was bowing.

The man on Clegg's right burst into raucous laughter and was followed by the man on Clegg's left. Clegg himself was in a cold sweat. He'd been tricked! They had pulled the oldest gag in the world on him, and now they were laughing in his face.

Clegg felt like a wounded lion. He wended his way through the crowd streaming toward the door and planted himself firmly in front of Bettel, who was gathering up the notes for his speech. Clegg berated him with admirable eloquence, reviled him, tore his speech to shreds. He went on for half an hour, nailing Bettel with his eyes, demolishing word by word the speaker's dialectical hypothesis, pulverizing it, annihilating it.

After he was through, Bettel clasped his hand warmly. "Sir," Bettel exclaimed, "your arguments are so persuasive that even I must agree with you. If you'd said this in front of all those people, you'd have ruined me."

Clegg turned around. The hall was empty. Everybody had gone home half an hour ago. The unhappy man shook his head. "Well, that's fifteen dollars down the drain," he sighed.

"You work for an agency?"

"Sure. Don't you?"

"Not me. I do it for the glory," Bettel replied. "Not so serious, I grant you, but I do make more money."

Septimius's adventure was much less complicated. He met the lady on the designated street corner, introduced himself politely, and offered her his arm. They murmured sweet nothings about fishing, the infernal Els, and the newest side show at Barnum's Circus. After a while a huge man burst out from behind a hedge and the lady whispered to Septimius, "Hit him in the ribs. His head's hard as rock."

But Septimius had ideas of his own. He hit the man instead square on the nose, belting him with such powerful punches that shortly he was off and running down the street to get his lawyer to start divorce proceedings. His face was covered with welts and looked like a potato.

"Will that do?" Septimius asked after the husband disappeared around the corner.

"Yes," the lady sighed, and threw herself into Septimius's arms. "I've always dreamed I'd find a brave, strong man like you . . ." This was a kink Septimius hadn't foreseen. He turned on his heel and fled down the street.

Clegg's fifteen plus Septimius's twenty-five, that made forty dollars down the drain. Well, to be precise: Clegg's fifteen and Septimius's twenty-five combined with Duncan's five hundred made five hundred forty dollars down the drain.

Duncan had shown up at the Imperial Hotel on time and asked for Mr. Striker. Mr. Striker received him in an office suite. Evidently Mr. Striker was a bigshot around the hotel. He was a man of few words. He eyed Duncan carefully and decided he was just the man for the job.

"Are you in any trouble with the police?" he asked. "Can you move around, show your face?"

"No trouble, free as a bird," Duncan reassured him, amused.

"Good. The work is easy but at the same time very involved. A certain person wants you to make friends with another person. This second person is in a big jam about money. Which helps you. The problem is, he's hard to track down and you've got to watch your step. I repeat, the job's clean as a whistle. You get in good with the second man, you make friends with him, build up his confidence in you, then you lead him into hot water that only the certain other person can get him out of. Use as much money as you need."

"You mean set it up for blackmail," Duncan deduced.

The man was put out. "Listen here, I'm no gangster. I'm Bill Striker and you can ask anybody who Bill Striker is. I'll be personally responsible for anything that happens to you. You'll see who Bill Striker is. How about it?"

"I accept tentatively," said Duncan. "When I find out just what this is all about, I'll give you my definite answer."

"Perfect. I'll tell you where to go for instructions right away."

Mr. Striker left the room and returned shortly. "Go up to the second floor. Suite 87. Knock at the door."

Duncan went up to Suite 87 and knocked. He was led into an elegant sitting room and waited for a few minutes. After a while a door opened and in came Clotilda Troll.

Clotilda turned pale, then blushed violently. Duncan

bowed politely. "Mr. Striker tells me that you are interested in my making friends with a person to get him in some kind of trouble. I've conditionally accepted the job. I'll decide when I hear the exact details. I'm at your service."

Clotilda sat down. Mr. Striker deserved to be slapped in the face. Trust me, he said, I'll find the right man for the job. Mr. Striker was a cretin, no doubt about it. The whole thing was ludicrous. Clotilda would have to tell him her plot. All right, Mr. Fitzmorris, you have to make friends with a certain Duncan Fitzmorris and lead him into a trap. There's no harm in it, Mr. Fitzmorris, all I want to do is to be able to say, Listen here, Duncan, either you get down on your knees and beg my forgiveness or it's back to the New York City jail.

Clotilda could have poisoned Mr. Striker. Of all the people in the world, he would have to come up with Duncan himself!

"I'm at your service," Duncan repeated. With that he put on his most impudent face. Clotilda didn't miss it and was about to burst into tears.

Why on earth hadn't that idiot Clegg warned her? She had to say something. So she did. "I'm terribly sorry, but I've changed my mind." Then she added with ill-concealed irritation: "Anyhow, you aren't suitable for the position. I need somebody with a great deal of intelligence."

"Thank you for the compliment," Duncan said, bowing.

After he closed the door behind himself, Clotilda began throwing knickknacks at the wall.

Paquebot, in his well-known *Histoires véritables,* narrates that the Prince of Kemel—whose legs, arms, and head had been shattered by mortar shards—when asked by General Dulubac how he was feeling, said, "Fine, thanks, and you?" There's no question that this was a singularly optimistic reply, but not nearly as cheerful as Duncan's to Septimius's and Clegg's query back at the hotel about how his day had gone.

"Superbly," said Duncan.

The truth of the matter was, he felt he'd said something very stupid. Clotilda was beginning to worry him. If that infernal girl was seriously in love with him, the whole business was becoming rather difficult. Maybe the best idea was to change his tack.

14

They had to earn some money, so the three gentlemen
went back to the agency. The fat man was in a rage.
"You fixed my wagon but good, didn't you! On account
of you, insults from Striker, insults from the bus company, insults from the lady. The streetcar company's
always trying to make the bus company look bad, and
you, Mr. Clegg, let them make a total moron out of
you! Then the lady with the divorce tells me Mr. North
won't marry her and she won't ever use my agency for
her divorces again. She's even going to make up with
the last husband so he'll come break my head." Then
he took on a philosophical tone. "Oh well, that's life
and bad organization. Water over the dam. Now I got
the perfect job for you three."

Peggy came in and smiled at Duncan.

"Involves a short trip to Cleveport," the fat man explained. "There you get in touch with the president of
a bona fide company. There's a sack of money in it for
you. Here's three train tickets and fifty bucks petty cash.
It's a clean job."

Duncan accepted. This was just what the doctor
ordered: to get out of New York City. The other two
gentlemen agreed immediately. They left the next day.
The trip was uneventful and in Cleveport they introduced themselves to the president of the company.

"The work I have for you," the president explained, "is simple but very delicate. My company is opening a gambling boat tomorrow night. We've outfitted a magnificent yacht, all the trimmings, very luxurious. We're calling it *Oasis in the Ocean*. At the appropriate moment, we'll bring out the gambling tables. The guests will come aboard in the evening, and we'll anchor twenty miles out. An island of light and life on the high seas. Music, dancing, drinks, dinner under the moon, and roulette, baccarat, blackjack until daybreak. It's going to be stupendous!"

In 1903, two years before, common law was repealed and a new law vigorously enforced in New York State. Not only did the new law prohibit working, selling, buying, target-shooting, hunting, fishing, horse-racing, and going to the theater or circus on Sunday, but it also prohibited gambling any day of the week. Anybody caught gambling was fined five times his winnings—or losses—during the twenty-four hour period. The owner of the gambling establishment would be fined a thousand dollars and sentenced to two years in prison. This explains the evolution of the floating gambling casino and why such a ship was destined to unparalleled success.

Duncan thought it was a fine idea, but he confessed he couldn't see where the three of them came into the picture.

The president laughed. "People are always suspicious of innovations and reluctant to get out their money. You will start them off right. Every night we'll provide you with several thousand dollars worth of chips and you'll pretend to be millionaires. You will gamble lavishly, lose and win with style, play a brilliant game. The croupiers and dealers will keep a close eye on you to avoid any unpleasant surprises when it comes time to cash your chips in. Ten dollars a day each, plus room and board and so forth. You're not allowed to gamble your own money."

The three gentlemen agreed, and their debut as shills on the glamorous yacht was superlative. They played with profound indifference, laughing gaily whenever they lost large piles of chips. They watched the wheels and cards with an air of sublime boredom. When the floating casino docked at Cleveport in the dawn, the president of the company congratulated Duncan, Septimius, and Clegg on their finesse. The second night the floating casino was packed. The third night even more people came. The fourth night they had to set up roulette wheels in the life boats.

Duncan on entering the casino found himself much admired, to say the least. It appeared that the most beautiful, the richest, the most elegant women in America had all congregated aboard the yacht. The cashier was frantically changing dollars into chips. Duncan played with the abandon of a billionaire. He lost, he won, he was supremely, elegantly bored. Toward midnight, he turned in an armload of chips for a hundred-thousand-dollar bill, went back to the roulette table, and put the bill on a number.

Instantly there was dead silence.

"I'm sorry, you can't do that," the croupier said. "If you win, we'll have to pay you three million six hundred thousand dollars. The house ceiling is three hundred sixty thousand."

Duncan smiled disdainfully. He called the manager over.

"We'll take the bet!" the manager shouted. Nobody in the room breathed.

The ball hurtled round and came to a halt. Twelve.

Duncan had put the banknote on twenty-five.

"Bring me some caviar and champagne from the buffet," Duncan ordered impassively. The waiter was staring at him, his mouth gaping. He wandered off stupidly. The whole room burst into applause.

"You were magnificent, Mr. Fitzmorris," a voice from behind whispered into Duncan's ear. "You're so blasé when you're spending other people's money." Clotilda sat down in front of him. Duncan didn't bat an eyelash.

"Your progress is astounding, Mr. Fitzmorris," Clotilda went on. "This line of work must pay a great deal more than Mrs. Thompson's seven dollars."

Duncan got up and went out on deck for a breath of fresh air. Clotilda padded silently after him. "You've picked a beautiful spot to ask me to forgive you for your dreary remarks on Mrs. Thompson's terrace," she whispered treacherously. "I'd be very upset if I had to tell all those nice people in there who the three of you really are. It would be quite ugly, all those angry Americans keelhauling you."

It was the most shameful blackmail. But Duncan wasn't flustered. "You say that I was rude to you on Mrs. Thompson's terrace?" he asked with astonishment. "That's odd. It's even incredible. Are you sure you're not mistaken? There must be more than one Fitzmorris in America. My great-grandfather's brother's family..."

"None of that," Clotilda said cheerfully. "I'm not mistaken. There's only one Fitzmorris like you in the world." Then, since she didn't want to be misunderstood, she added, "Fortunately."

"Very odd," said Duncan, turning his back on the ocean and looking toward the casino. "Really an extraordinary situation," he said, but in a different tone of voice. Then, grasping Clotilda firmly around the waist, he picked her up and threw her overboard.

Let us step forward in time and quote verbatim an article which appeared in every American newspaper the day after Clotilda fell overboard.

For some time a large group of landowners and industrialists from New York City and environs have been entertained on a new, elegant "floating nightclub," owned and operated aboard a large yacht by a Cleveport corporation.

Last night the floating nightclub *Oasis in the Ocean* weighed anchor from Cleveport booked to capacity. At midnight the ship was 80 miles offshore. Amid festivities, the waiters, croupiers, dealers, manager and crew drew out pistols and ordered guests to hand over money and jewelry. The guests were then imprisoned in the hold while the pirates, loaded with booty, deserted the yacht and fled at full speed in three cabin cruisers. Observers say that *Oasis in the Ocean* was not a nightclub at all but a gambling casino. It is therefore assumed that the guests sustained considerable losses.

This explains Duncan's violent act. Duncan had not lost his usual control, as one might have interpreted it. Though his desire to throw Clotilda overboard must have been immense, Clotilda actually wound up in the water only because Duncan, glancing at the glass doors to the casino room, had seen the counterfeit croupiers and waiters pull out their guns.

Just after Clotilda hit the water Duncan followed her in. Clotilda was thrashing around trying to free herself from her long evening skirt when Duncan grabbed hold of her by the hair and began swimming toward the stern. Four large cabin cruisers were ready and waiting, their motors idling as they rode the waves. Duncan climbed aboard one, dragged Clotilda ungracefully after him, cast off the lines, took the helm and pushed the throttle full ahead.

The moon had disappeared behind a mass of black clouds and they steamed along blindly and silently for a while. Clotilda didn't open her mouth. She too had seen what was happening in the gambling room. There was no point in asking for an explanation. But finally she couldn't control herself any longer. "Thanks for saving me from the pirates," she said very sarcastically.

Duncan didn't answer. He simply turned the wheel and began to circle back toward the now distant *Oasis in the Ocean.*

"No, Mr. Fitzmorris!" Clotilda squeaked. "I meant it as a joke!"

Duncan put the boat back on course. On and on blindly and silently, until finally the boat ran into something solid. There was no point now in trying to navigate. All they could do was get out and walk. Clotilda, shivering with the cold, followed Duncan in silence.

Once over a wall of boulders, the two castaways found themselves on a flat expanse, watching the sun rise. "Oh, no!" exclaimed Duncan. "We're on Bess Island again!"

"Be my guest," laughed Clotilda, who on solid ground had found her tongue. "It's sweet of you to have saved me from pirates and escorted me home."

15

They reached the villa as the sun was rising. One of the windows came open easily. Inside, a scent of jasmine still hung in the air, but Clotilda didn't make any witty remarks about blond countesses. Their clothes had been soaked through, and the first project was to dig up some dry ones. When Duncan, nattily dressed in one of Mr. Troll's few remaining suits, finally made his way downstairs again, he found Clotilda repossessed of all her poise, elegance, and impudence.

"Your shoulders, Mr. Fitzmorris, are magnificent," said Clotilda. "I've never seen two shoulders to be compared with them."

Duncan didn't answer but Clotilda went on about his shoulders. "I've seen the sun set over the Matterhorn," said Clo, "but even that couldn't hold a candle to your shoulders."

Duncan got up and stood in front of the girl, with his feet firmly apart. "Miss Troll," he began, "for a long time I had the good taste and luck not to know you existed. You've wormed your way into my life with diabolical system. You've thrust me into a distasteful mess. In fact, for some time now you've tried to make my life as difficult as possible. Now would you like to tell me why you went to all this trouble?"

"I thought I already told you, on Mrs. Thompson's terrace," Clo answered.

Then she regretted saying it. It occurred to her that she was no longer on Mrs. Thompson's terrace. She was on a microscopic island lost in the Atlantic, alone with a man. To be precise, she was alone with Duncan. For the first time in her life Clotilda felt vaguely afraid. She shot Duncan a worried look and could have sworn she saw the trace of a strange smile on his lips.

"We'll discuss this more calmly later, Mr. Fitzmorris," she said with as much cheek as she could muster. "Now I want to rest." Clotilda went off to lock herself in her room, barricading the door with furniture. Around midday she reappeared, fresh, calm, and smiling. "Do you intend to allow me the pleasure of your company very long, Mr. Fitzmorris?" Clotilda asked.

Duncan was speechless for a moment. "Well, really, I would leave if I could," he explained. "The trouble is, I don't quite know how to leave. It's not as if there's a ferry service between Bess and New York."

"True," Clo admitted. "It's a shame, though. Why don't you take a stroll over to the dune you ran that boat aground on and figure out whether it's salvageable?"

Duncan went to have a look at the boat. The biggest piece was about the size of a saucer, and with the best intentions in the world he might possibly make a stool out of the debris. But how was a stool going to get him out of this predicament? Duncan returned to the villa perplexed.

The door and windows were tightly shut. He knocked politely and then tried to force the shutters.

"It's pointless," came a voice from above. Clotilda was watching him, amused, from a crack in one of the upstairs shutters. "Don't waste your strength. Everything's barred and I've got furniture barricading the windows and doors."

"What do you mean by this?" Duncan shouted up to her.

"I mean that this is my house and I receive whom I choose to receive. I make the rules. Since I can't get you off my island, I won't let you in my house. Now if you'll excuse me, Mr. Fitzmorris, I'm going to have lunch. The cellar's full of food and I'm just ravenous."

This was the beginning of the most original siege in this story: the most original only because the besieged party was outside the fortress under the bright blue sky.

Duncan was hungry as a wolf. From time to time Clotilda came to the window. "You can't imagine how good these biscuits and caviar taste. And this ham!" Clotilda communicated to him. Or: "There are still people in the world who make an art of bottling partridge. You should taste it!"

This was the second embargo Duncan had been put under on Bess Island. He'd managed to survive the first brilliantly. But that had involved only a lady smuggler and twenty outlaws. This involved Clotilda.

Toward nightfall Clotilda reappeared and dictated the conditions for surrender. "The sky is clouding over," she said. "Evidently there's going to be a hurricane to-night. A real rockbuster. It will be too bad for anybody out in it. If you'd like a nice solid roof over your head, warm bedcovers, lots of good food, all you have to do is humbly beg my pardon—*very* humbly—for your despicable behavior on Mrs. Thompson's terrace."

Duncan sat on the ground and recalled an episode from the glorious history of the Fitzmorris family. "My paternal great-great-grandfather," said Duncan, "in 1771 was thrown in a dungeon by the Duke of Bourneton, who told him that he'd be fed when he agreed to one thing. Twelve days later, rather impressed that my great-great-grandfather had given no sign of surrender even though he hadn't had nourishment in all that time, the duke paid him a visit. Is there anything I can do for you, Lord Fitzmorris? the duke asked. Yes, said my great-great-grandfather. You would do me a great favor if you brought me a decent physic. I've a dreadful belly-ache. —Now does that give you some idea of the Fitzmorris attitude toward economic sanctions and blackmail?" Duncan concluded.

"In that case, sleep well," Clotilda said as she pulled the shutter to.

It never did rain, but when he woke up the next morning, Duncan was freezing to death. The sun was rising and Clotilda poked her head out the window. "Beautiful day, isn't it, Mr. Fitzmorris?" she inquired.

"Splendid, Miss Troll."

"Did you sleep well?"

"Magnificently. Comes of having a clear conscience."

Clotilda described her breakfast and the richness of the biscuits. At lunchtime she described the exquisite tuna and pickle salad she'd made. Dinnertime brought another description and another suggestion that he surrender. Duncan was faint with hunger but found enough strength to tell her another story about his family's exceptional powers of resistance.

From that point on, Clotilda changed her conditions for surrender. She wanted, in addition to humble apologies, a declaration of love in verse, signed and dated. She wanted her friends in New Islip to have a good laugh. Duncan refused haughtily and Clotilda sighed with relief for the second time.

After his second bout with the cold under the stars, Duncan woke up a little addled. He hadn't eaten for fifty-six hours.

"How on earth did my great-great-grandfather manage for twelve days?" Duncan asked himself. "Only fifty-six hours without food and already I'm dying."

He was so weak that, ancestors or no ancestors, he was about to give in. *Two* declarations of love in verse, but he had to eat. He waited for the usual window to open. Instead the door flew open and out came Clotilda. She was very pale and looked as if she'd been crying.

Duncan was amazed. Was it possible? Had he won? Again?

"I'm hungry, Duncan," Clo wailed. "I haven't eaten for fifty-six hours. I couldn't find so much as a cracker!"

"What about your descriptions of succulent partridge?"

Clo shrugged her shoulders soundlessly. Duncan spread his arms. "What can I do about it?" he said. "It's been fifty-six hours since the last time I saw a bite of food too."

"But it runs in your family!" Clotilda wailed. "You've got all those ancestors who require physics after starving for twelve days! I'm not used to it! The Troll family die of hunger after two days without food!"

"What if I'd surrendered to your descriptions?" Duncan asked.

"I'd still have been hungry, but I would have had the satisfaction," Clotilda explained.

Duncan didn't strangle Clotilda. He just went inside. He peered into every crevice without avail. Then he remembered the nights they had spent in the kitchen with the smugglers. Septimius had crammed the sofa full of foodstuffs. Duncan raised the cushions, and between the springs he uncovered an enormous cache of bottles and tins.

Clotilda was outside the villa, wailing. Duncan closed the door and threw the bolts. He opened a few tins, uncorked a bottle, and carried them upstairs to one of the windows.

"There are still people in the world who make an art of bottling partridge," he exclaimed as he began to wolf down the contents of the tins.

Clotilda sprang up and looked at him, hallucinated. Then she threw herself against the door.

"Save your strength," Duncan warned her. "It's barred. You can't imagine how delicious this caviar on biscuit tastes. The best," he added.

Clotilda looked at him desperately, wringing her hands. "I'll have you arrested for trespassing and theft!" she howled.

Clotilda threw herself on the ground and began to weep pitifully, more from anger than from hunger. That afternoon, as he finished a huge meal at the window, Duncan dictated his conditions for surrender.

"If you don't want to die of hunger on this infernal sand dune, you will write what I dictate and sign it."

"It's blackmail, it's unfair," said Clotilda without moving, "but I'll do it."

Duncan lowered pen, ink, and paper down on a string. When Clo was ready, he began dictating.

To the captain of the Dolphin:
I order you to take on board Messrs. Duncan Fitzmor-ris, Septimius North, and Barton Clegg whenever they request it, for whatever purpose, and wherever they choose to go.

Clotilda Troll

The letter in hand, Duncan let Clotilda in and she finally had something to eat. She ate heroically, not like any ordinary starving girl. She had great style. One might even say she ate with pride.

After she finished, Duncan approached her. "A Fitz-morris," he said solemnly, "needs no help to get home." He took Clo's letter out of his pocket and tore it to shreds.

Clotilda smiled. "The day you write me to beg my pardon, I will not tear your letter up. It would be such a shame to waste the words of a Fitzmorris in love!"

Duncan studied her face. "Good lord," he said, spreading his arms in supplication, "why does a good-looking girl like you have to be such a witch?"

"I'm flattered by your comments on my physical appearance," said Clo as she ran to barricade herself in her room.

Night had fallen on Bess Island. In point of fact, night had fallen elsewhere as well, and the moon had come up over the water, creating a most romantic scene. For that reason Clotilda, seated in front of her bedroom window, felt unbearably sad. She watched the moon's reflection in the endless ocean and was sad primarily because she couldn't figure one thing out. "Now then," Clo thought, "when I'm face to face with Duncan, I love and hate him at the same time. But when he's out of sight, I can only love him. I wonder why that is?"

At the same time Duncan was staring out his window, thinking thoughts no less serious. "I'm in a pickle," he thought. "If this loathsome girl really is in love with me and it's not the joke I thought it was to begin with, then it must be serious. I could declare war on the whole United States, but I cannot fight a millionairess in love. This despicable girl is going to work out plan after diabolical plan to put me on the spot where I have to choose between ruin or surrender on her terms."

It was a tragic situation. Either drink the castor oil and inherit his two million pounds, and thus defend himself against Clo's plots, or remain exposed to the peril of having to marry Clotilda, that infernal Clotilda. If Clotilda was in love with him, that meant every wretched plan she had was aimed at getting him to marry her. At a certain point Duncan ceased to think logically. To marry Clotilda in order not to be forced (the point was to protect himself against the plague of Clotilda's devilish schemes) to drink the glass of castor oil was certainly not the only solution.

Duncan worried about his predicament as he stared at the sea shimmering under the moonlight. Then he decided. "No, a thousand times better to perjure myself than marry that asinine girl!"

He would have to do it politely, though, not rush things. Duncan went to bed with his plan worked out, while Clotilda put out her lamp and tucked herself in, concluding: "That arrogant fathead *is* going to marry me, if I have to get him to do it at the point of a gun!"

16

The next day Clotilda and Duncan found themselves back in New York, after the usual trite story of two castaways signaling to a passing ship. They were taken to the Port Authority police and a sergeant interrogated them. How had they gotten to Bess Island?

Clotilda began the story. "I was on board a floating nightclub when suddenly the hired help pulled out guns. Since I was on deck, I dived into the water. There was a cabin cruiser tied to the stern and I . . ."

The police sergeant interrupted her with a whoop of triumph. "You must be Clotilda Troll! We thought the gangsters had kidnapped you for ransom and all the policemen in the States are on the alert looking for you. Thank God you're alive!"

After making a dozen phone calls he turned back to them. "Who's the gentleman with you?"

"I haven't the remotest," Clotilda said with all the face she had. "When I arrived at Bess I found him on the beach looking like a drowned rat. He said he'd been in a shipwreck. I gave him some old clothes of my father's. That's all I know about him."

Duncan went into a cold sweat. He had no papers, the police had already booked him once: he hadn't a prayer of being believed. Clotilda had the knife in his back again. Duncan clenched his teeth and began inventing the sad tale of a castaway.

"I don't get the picture at all," said the sergeant. "We'll have to detain you for questioning."

Before he was taken away by two policemen, Duncan found time to bow and whisper something in Clo's ear. "Thanks for arranging for a nice warm room for me again. I'll remember to leave you to drown the next time."

"Aside from the fact that you threw me into the water," Clo answered, smiling, "you ought to be grateful to me. If I'd told the truth, the sweet fact that you were those pirates' accomplice would have come out. Just the same, I shall come to visit you, Mr. Fitzmorris. Do you have set days to receive visitors or doesn't it make any difference?"

Clotilda watched with some satisfaction as Duncan was led off. "At least now I know where to find him," she thought happily. "And this way I know he's not in danger."

When Duncan heard the bolts shot into place on the door of his second prison cell, he felt very depressed. More than anything he felt remorse. He should have left Clotilda to drown. He bitterly regretted his failure to do so, but it was too late now. Who was going to help him out of this fix? He was completely at Clotilda's mercy. Even if Septimius and Clegg were still wandering around America, how could they possibly find him?

Duncan was not, however, expecting the American newspapers to come to his rescue. He spent an unpleasant night, but in the morning a welcome surprise was awaiting him. He was told that there was somebody to see him and he was led out to the visitors' room. Septimius had found him.

He was very agitated: he explained that the night before every newspaper was filled with stories about the reappearance of the missing millionairess Clotilda Troll. And about the arrest of a highly suspect castaway who called himself Duncan Fitzmorris. After that, it had been no problem tracking him down. Even Clotilda had had the sense to observe that it was no problem to find a man in prison.

Septimius asked him what he could do. "Mr. Fitzmorris," Septimius stammered with emotion, "if you like, I'll get myself arrested to keep you company."

"Thanks, but that's not necessary," said Duncan. "Instead write to my lawyer under my name and ask Dickson to come here with the glass of castor oil and the two witnesses. All expenses paid, of course. Make it fast. This is urgent."

Septimius's face lit up. "You mean you've decided to obey your mother's wishes?"

"With all due respect to my mother," Duncan answered, "let's not have it said that I'm giving in to her wishes yet. This is only a precaution. You'll see."

Before Septimius left, Duncan asked after Clegg. Septimius blushed and hung his head. Duncan clutched at the bars separating him from his visitor. "What's happened?" he asked, worried.

Septimius lifted a large sack he had propped up in the corner and held it open. It was Clegg's wooden leg.

"What have you done with the rest of him?"

"He's at the hotel," Septimius explained. "I caught Mr. Clegg writing a note to Clotilda Troll and made him confess."

Dungan glared at him.

"No, no, Mr. Fitzmorris," Septimius hurried to assure him. "I promise I hit him very softly, as if he were my own brother! Clegg is in Miss Troll's pay. He tipped her off when we were going to Mrs. Thompson's, then when we were on that gambling boat. I keep an eye on him day and night. When I go out I take his leg with me so he can't move off his bed."

Duncan burst into guffaws and then fervently shook Septimius's big hand. "Thanks, my friend!" Then he went back to meditate in his cell.

The next day they led him into the visitors' room and he found Clotilda waiting for him. "Sorry not to have waited for you to invite me," she apologized, smiling, "but I just had to know how you were adapting to your new surroundings."

"Superbly," Duncan reassured her. "I feel much safer now that prison walls protect me from you."

Clotilda was looking particularly well that morning. She asked politely if the view from the windows of his flat was good, how long he would be staying in his present accommodations, and if he had plans for redecoration.

Duncan wasn't fooled. He was waiting for the knife to be thrust. Then it came. "I must in all decency warn you, Mr. Fitzmorris," she sighed, "that things don't look too good for you. It seems that our adventure with the smugglers has come out, evidently the ship you said had been shipwrecked turned up yesterday without a scratch, et cetera. I'd advise you to hire a good lawyer. Lawyers here are very costly but in cases like this you should spare no expense."

Duncan nodded in agreement.

"I've found the perfect lawyer for you," Clotilda went on. "I suggest you put everything in his hands. His name is Smithson, a very good solicitor who will arrange things in three days. I'll take your case to him myself, if you like."

"I'm very grateful, Miss Troll," Duncan answered.

"Very good," Clo said. "All you have to do is give me a check for three thousand dollars. Smithson won't take a case without a retainer. Rather crass, these American lawyers, but what can you do?"

Duncan held out his hands helplessly. "I'm sorry, but at the moment I'm not in a position to be able to give you that check. It will be some time before I'll have a checking account. The slow process of bank bureaucracy, you know."

"What a shame!" said Clo. "In a week your case will be much more serious. You know I would help you, Mr. Fitzmorris, but you understand . . . What would people think of this sort of interest on my part? You know yellow journalism here in America. They'll make a scandal out of anything. The fact that we were on the island alone together for a few days has set tongues wagging and my reputation is still intact only because I had the presence of mind to say I didn't know you when we were picked up. But if I take up your cause now, what will become of me? People always gossip about a woman who takes interest in a man who's not her husband . . . Now, if you were my husband, that would be a different story."

"True," observed Duncan, sighing. "The trouble is, though, I'm not your husband. In any case they can only hang me."

"Isn't that sufficient?"

"Well, of course it's a nuisance, but it's better than marrying you."

"I won't disturb you any longer," Clotilda finished, smiling. "I'll come to see you in a couple of months."

Duncan was bored beyond endurance during the twenty days that followed his interview with Clotilda. Finally he was taken to the visitors' room and found

Septimius with his lawyer Dickson and the two witnesses.

The lawyer greeted Duncan coldly. He was of the strictly conventional genre of solicitors who prefer to ignore clients who find their way into jail, even if a foreign jail. The lawyer carried a briefcase. He set it on the table, opened it, took out a metal container and from the container the glass of castor oil.

"Here, Mr. Fitzmorris," the lawyer said. "Let us pray it does your body and soul good."

Duncan shook his head, smiling. There was no need to rush things. He would set a date for the ceremony later, and in the meantime the lawyer and two witnesses were to remain in New York. Mr. North would see to it that their stay was comfortable.

"But I must . . ." the dignified solicitor began.

"You will receive from my departed mother everything necessary to reimburse you for your trouble. I recall that the fund for the execution of the will is unlimited. Isn't there a clause to that effect?"

"Yes, but . . ." the lawyer continued to babble.

"The estate amounts to some two million pounds, doesn't it?" asked Duncan. Then he pointed out that was sufficient to sustain several generations of lawyers.

The lawyer, the two witnesses, and Septimius left. Duncan returned to his cell. He would drink it, yes, but not until he couldn't tolerate things as they were any longer.

Duncan managed to stand it for a whole month more. Then he decided that there were two possible solutions: either go insane, or marry Clotilda, or drink the castor oil. *Two* possibilities, since going insane and marrying Clotilda were one and the same thing.

Every morning the lawyer and the two witnesses showed up and waited for Duncan to give the word.

"Tomorrow," Duncan would say. The thirtieth day he knew tomorrow really would be the day. He had spent another wretched night. He had dreamed all his ancestors had condemned him in disgust. Then he had dreamed of a river of castor oil in which two thousand Clotildas were swimming around. At eight o'clock, sitting on his cot with his head between his hands, he was thinking that in one hour he would be the first Fitzmorris ever to surrender.

The cell door opened. "You're wanted in the visitors' lounge," the warden announced.

Duncan went down as if on his way to the gallows, but as soon as he arrived in the visitors' room his heart leaped with joy.

"You, Peggy?" he stammered, staring amazed at the gorgeous girl from the agency.

"We're awfully sorry," Peggy said with deep concern, "that you got into this jam on account of us. But neither Dick nor I have forgotten about you."

Duncan smiled and bowed. "All my problems are much relieved by the sight of your beautiful face," he declared. Peggy was obviously very flattered.

"Mr. Fitzmorris," she explained in a low voice, "we haven't forgotten you and we've found a marvelous job for you. You could earn a packet of money."

Duncan shook his head sadly. "Thanks for thinking of me," he answered, "but I'm afraid this time I can't work for you. It's not that I don't want to but I think the warden might be opposed to the idea. He has a rather pigheaded notion about not letting his guests move around too much."

"Mr. Fitzmorris," Peggy begged, "please be serious. Smithson, the most famous lawyer in New York State, needs a bright young assistant. He hasn't had a good case for a while and the papers don't mention him much any more. Smithson asked our advice and of course we thought of you."

Duncan blinked. "But what could I possibly do for Smithson?" he objected.

"Let yourself be condemned, that's all," Peggy explained.

Duncan was stupefied and began shaking his head. But Peggy reassured him. "It's a breeze. Other people have done it before and come through free as birds. Smithson will take care of everything. He'll have you accused of a crime you couldn't possibly have committed, he'll let them make a lot of noise about it, then he'll defend you and win a great victory over miscarriage of justice. It's very simple, Mr. Fitzmorris. The D.A.'s case will fall apart and you'll go free and receive a lot of money besides. Smithson will even put it in writing, if you want."

Now he had three choices: marry Clotilda, drink the castor oil, or risk his neck. Duncan chose without hesitation.

"I'll do it, Peggy. I'm at Smithson's orders and I'll be expecting his instructions."

"I knew you'd do it," Peggy exclaimed joyfully. "For the moment, don't do anything except say you know nothing."

"Will you tell me what I'll be accused of?"

"I don't know," said Peggy. "What difference does it make?"

"Just curiosity," Duncan said.

Peggy left after she had blown Duncan a kiss through the bars.

When a few moments later the lawyer arrived with the two witnesses, Duncan put him off as usual. "Mr. Dickson, just be patient. We'll discuss it another day."

17

The moment Peggy hung up after telling Smithson everything was set, the lawyer called his secretary. "We got him to do it," he announced. "Let's get to work."

The New York Police Department had thirty or so unsolved crimes on its books, the most spectacular of which was referred to as the "Upstate Express Heist."

The Upstate Express had departed on the evening of May 25, 1905, from Grand Central Terminal with forty-five cars. It had arrived in Buffalo with forty-four. It's not an unusual thing to have a car, that is, the *last* car, come uncoupled and left stranded on the track. The odd thing was, the missing one didn't happen to be the last car. It had been the twenty-fifth. That is, the *middle* car. No clues had come to light since the twenty-fifth of May, either about the car or about its thirty passengers. Naturally the police department hadn't been able to do a thing. The car was discovered missing at Elmira. There was no stop between New York and Elmira. In other words, a sensational, insoluble mystery. Smithson of course decided to have Duncan accused of masterminding the Upstate Express Heist.

When Smithson visited Duncan to explain his plan, Duncan shook his head. "I don't see how it can work," he objected. "It's not in my character to steal a railroad car with thirty passengers aboard. That's something only a well-equipped gang could manage."

"I'm not so sure," the lawyer said. "You wouldn't need that many people."

Duncan laughed. "Don't be silly, Mr. Smithson. It would require at least three men on the train, one man on the track as sentry, one at the switch to the spur, five to uncouple and recouple the cars. Then men posted throughout the rest of the train, and so forth."

The lawyer shrugged his shoulders. "I think you're wrong, but it's your decision. I'll find something less involved to hang on you."

The lawyer left the prison apparently frothing at the mouth. But when he got to his office he told his secretary otherwise: "We're in business, Mickey." Then he dictated a letter to the Chief of the State Police:

> *If you want to know how the Upstate Express Heist was pulled, ask a prisoner named Duncan Fitzmorris in the Fifth Precinct Jail. If you're smart you'll lead him to believe that you think the heist was engineered by one person, so as not to arouse his suspicions.*
>
> *A Friend of Justice*

When the Chief of Police received the note, he called in Mr. Pew, the best detective on the force, and handed it over to him. "This might be from some nut, but you'd better follow it up just in case. Watch your step."

The next day Duncan acquired a cellmate. Duncan was happy to see him. He'd been alone long enough to welcome any new face, even this painfully ugly one, who was at least companionable and chatty. Their conversations were interesting; Duncan found himself discussing the latest news and of course they touched on the Upstate Express Heist. The new prisoner had the wild idea that the car had been hijacked by one man.

This irritated Duncan. "I can see how some tyro might believe such drivel," he exclaimed, "but from you, a self-confessed professional thief, it's incredible!"

The professional thief protested, and then, very put out, he shouted, "You say it would have taken a whole army. All right, where are you going to put all of them?"

Duncan developed his theory carefully. "Three men stationed in the designated car. You're after the middle car, so it's particularly touchy. One man stays inside the car to signal through the window to his accomplices waiting in the night to ambush the train. The other two men station themselves on the front and rear platforms respectively. They loosen the couplings so the car can be detached in a hurry when the time comes.

"Meanwhile, a lot of fake track workers install a hand switch, lay a 'detour' coming off the main track which will lead eventually to two sturdy wagons in the vicinity. One man is posted at the switch. Another lies face down as close as possible to the junction between the spur and the main track.

"At the appropriate moment the men on the car platforms uncouple it. The man inside sticks his lamp out the window and signals as planned. Due to the speed of the train, at first nothing is noticeable. But the cars will slowly drift apart, so that when they reach the spur there will be enough time to allow the designated car to turn off and still to throw the switch back in place before the second section of train catches up. The man lying near the track will control the split-second timing with his light signals.

"Then, as the train chugs off toward its destination, our car rolls down the spur. The man on the rear platform enters the car and he and the lamp man keep order at gunpoint. The fellow on the front platform acts as brakeman and slows the car down so that it just glides gently to a stop on the wagon. Furthermore, you need eight wooden blocks to wedge under the wheels, half a dozen good-size waterproof canvases to cover the whole thing, four whiplashes, and your horses are trotting away with your package neatly sealed, special delivery. As that wagon goes off, all the rest of the gang occupies itself taking up the spur track, restoring the area to its natural state, loading the track and ties aboard the other wagon, and then they head off for wherever they'd planned to meet.

"There you are. Simple, isn't it?"

"Simple as pie. But how do you know so much about it?"

"Know?" Duncan replied, laughing. "I don't *know* anything. It's just an educated guess."

"You're a nice guy," the professional thief said sadly. "Which is a shame, because there've been two stenographers sitting outside the door taking down every word you said."

"That *is* a shame," Duncan complained. "If I'd known that, I would have developed my theory with a little more style, made it juicier."

"Don't give a thought to your style!" the professional thief laughed. "We don't go in much for style." Then he introduced himself. "Pew, Detective, Fifth Precinct."

When Pew had gone, Duncan began to laugh with genuine amusement. "Some solicitor," he said to himself. "He not only fooled the police, he completely pulled the wool over my eyes. Well, I'd better take this like a respectable Fitzmorris and resign myself to being the mastermind of the Upstate Express Heist."

So when they began interrogating him a few hours later about where he'd hidden the car and thirty passengers, Duncan just babbled nervously that he knew nothing, he was innocent.

Naturally, some accomplices were called for and Smithson rang the agency to ask if they had any likely candidates. "Mr. Fitzmorris's two friends might do," Peggy suggested. "They're staying at the Brighton. Why don't you have them arrested?"

Another anonymous note to the police chief and Clegg and Septimius were shaken out of bed and marched off to jail. The inquest went feverishly. The smuggling episode, the first arrest, the release on bail, all helpfully condemning, were brought out.

Then it came to light that bail for the three men had been put up by Clotilda Troll. There it was, clearly on record. Now why had Miss Clotilda Troll gone five thousand dollars out of her way to help these three mysterious criminals? And how had Clotilda Troll come across Fitzmorris on Bess Island? And what had made her say she'd never seen him before when she'd been the one to post his bail? Information gleaned from their consulate revealed them all as persons of the highest social position. But that meant nothing. Or rather, didn't it doubtless mean that Fitzmorris, bored with his life of millionaire's ease, had plotted to vent his spleen by hiring Clegg and North to traverse the Atlantic to pull a train heist with him?

The three of them insisted they'd been on Bess from the nineteenth to the twenty-ninth of May. Who could corroborate this alibi? The fact that they'd landed in New York the night of the twenty-ninth and had had themselves arrested—wasn't that an obvious ruse to establish their alibi? The newspapers ran this sort of headline: MILLIONAIRE FITZMORRIS HIJACKS TRAIN CAR, PASSENGERS. WHAT BECAME OF THIRTY INNOCENT PASSEN-

GERS? Finally one paper ran this lead piece: WHY HASN'T CLOTILDA TROLL BEEN ARRESTED?

Georgie, soaking up some jazz and an ice-cream soda at a Seventh Avenue delicatessen with his countess, spotted one of these headlines, bought the paper, and proceeded to get very nervous. "Kitty," he said, "this is dreadful!"

Kitty sighed. "You're right. It's disastrous. I've been following it all along and I'm so sad not to be able to help them."

"Yes," Georgie agreed, "but there must be something we can do. I mean, you can't just leave somebody in a mess like this."

Gorgeous, seductive, delicious Kitty shook her head. "Can you think of a way to stage an escape for anybody they're making that much noise about?"

Georgie blinked. "Do you mean to say they've already thrown Clotilda in jail?"

The beautiful smuggler grasped that she'd said something rather tactless and rushed to patch things up. "I thought you were talking about Duncan," she said. "I can't imagine Miss Troll in that kind of a mess."

Georgie handed Kitty the newspaper. "Read that, Kitty. They're clamoring to have Clotilda arrested!" he exclaimed. "Wouldn't you say that was a bad enough mess for any girl?"

Kitty pretended to be very concerned and shocked about Clotilda's situation. The fact was, she couldn't have cared less about Clotilda. But there was no point in arguing with Georgie. So when he decided they must run to the aid of Clo, she agreed enthusiastically.

"What a pleasant surprise!" Clotilda exclaimed at

Georgie's and Kitty's appearance. "I'll bet you two came to tell me you're getting married."

"Clo," said Georgie solemnly, "we're here to offer you our help. Kitty, too—that is, Countess de la Sierra."

"How kind of you, Countess. But right now I've no intention of going into the opium business."

Clotilda loathed and detested Kitty. The details Clegg wouldn't tell her about the sojourn on Bess made her supremely irritable every time she thought about them. This was why she raised the question of opium. Georgie evidently knew nothing about women, because he fully expected Kitty to faint dead away at the mention of the word opium. Kitty, however, showed no emotion at all. "Each to her own sort of contraband," she threw back. "Countesses smuggle opium, million-airesses shanghai men. No doubt you're salty because I managed to wind up with both cargoes."

"You sacked my house!" Clotilda screamed. "You pose as a Spanish countess! You lead this fat imbecile around by the nose! And now you have the face to offer to help *me!* I should have you arrested on the spot!"

"If my eyes don't deceive me," Kitty pointed out, "the New York papers aren't after any countess, they're out to get your hide. Here, have a look for yourself."

Clotilda gave a deprecatory shrug. "A pack of lies," she said disdainfully. "I'll simply sue all the papers. How could I possibly have had a hand in Mr. Fitzmorris's scheming? Or have been involved in his train robbery and kidnapping of thirty passengers? He'll have to answer for all these rich man's whims of his."

Kitty was livid. "You are one of the most hateful women I have ever known," she asserted. "Because of some half-witted prank of yours, a man is in serious trouble—three men, in fact—and you have the gall to say that. How could Duncan have had anything to do with that robbery when you know perfectly well he was on Bess Island with *me* on the twenty-fifth of May?"

"And what was he doing there?" Clotilda said innocently.

Kitty blushed but didn't give up. "He did anything he pleased and there are twenty-one witnesses who will swear to that."

"I don't know how valid the court would consider the testimonies of twenty-one opium smugglers," Clotilda remarked. "And then I don't think any smuggler would be very keen to appear before a court of law to help three gentlemen."

"Unlike gentlemen," Kitty said proudly, "smugglers can permit themselves the luxury of telling the truth at least once in their life."

"You make me laugh!" Clotilda exclaimed.

But Kitty was not going to let herself be flustered. "There's no law against insane millionairesses laughing," she said. "But I don't know how any law can condone an insane millionairess who kidnaps three men and hides them away. It wouldn't be too hard to find the crew of your *Dolphin*. If I'm not mistaken, it's docked here. And they'd squeal, take my word for it."

Georgie planted himself in an armchair and kept his mouth shut. Clotilda had already exhausted her key arguments. She had one left, of inferior quality to be sure, but that was beside the point. "All right," she cried. "I have good reason for whatever I do to Mr. Fitzmorris. But why are *you* meddling with him?"

"For precisely the same reason you are," Kitty said hotly.

At this point Georgie put a word in. He shrugged his shoulders and said disconsolately, "Well, the truth will out. You're in love with Duncan too."

Kitty turned to him. "No, Georgie," she amended.

"That's not quite right. She's only in love with Duncan, whereas I love you too."

"Well, thank God for that," he sighed, relieved. "It's a step in the right direction. If someday the good lord sends me a woman that isn't in love with Duncan and loves only me, my gratitude will have no bounds."

When Kitty and Georgie had gone, Clotilda ran out to see Smithson the lawyer. Smithson was in a foul mood and wouldn't let Clotilda begin grilling him. "Miss Troll," he said blackly, "I have done everything you asked me to. I fooled Peggy, that girl from the agency, I hoodwinked the police, I managed to get Fitzmorris into a jam only you can get him out of. But the thing's out of hand completely. I have no control any more. Your name has come into it too, Miss Troll, and I assure you none of this has been my fault."

"I understand," said Clotilda. "The only trouble is, it keeps growing and growing and soon I'll be arrested. Then the whole business about the *Dolphin* joke and the Bess Island kidnapping and my name will be smeared all over the front page."

"No, it's not very pretty," Smithson admitted. "They've had it up to here with European millionaires. It's common knowledge that you all come over here just to have a good laugh at the expense of the American public. It's parvenu jealousy of the European establishment. And now they suspect you came over here to make fun of our American laws as well."

"Very perspicacious of them," Clotilda said sarcastically, and went on to tell him about her scene with Kitty. Smithson promised to keep Kitty at bay. Then Clo asked how Duncan was behaving himself.

"I warned him not to say anything, and he hasn't," the lawyer told her. "He won't clarify anything he said before, he's playing dumb. He's confident everything will turn out all right, so he's having a lot of fun."

"He'd have a lot more fun, that blockhead, if I were thrown in jail too," Clo howled. Then she dried her tears and whimpered, "How dreadful for him, to be shut up in prison forever."

18

For several weeks now Dickson and the two witnesses visited Duncan faithfully every morning to offer him through the bars the castor oil which, distasteful as it was, could save him. One affirmative sigh from Duncan and the late Mrs. Fitzmorris, who was watching Duncan's every move from her cloud in the sky, would have been able to say to her husband, who shared the same cloud, "What did I tell you, dear?" The late Mr. and Mrs. Fitzmorris, seated on their cloud, talked about Duncan often. Mr. Fitzmorris had long disapproved of Mrs. Fitzmorris's action.

"Your behavior toward our son, my dear, has always appeared to me particularly reprehensible. To disinherit Duncan out of spite was profoundly unjust."

"Let me point out a grave error in your statement," Mrs. Fitzmorris would answer. "*I* never disinherited him. I had a clause put in the will which I believed to be to his benefit."

"Women use the strangest logic," Mr. Fitzmorris would answer. "If that were not the case, how could you define such a clause as beneficial, since it condemns him to perpetual poverty? I know my son. He's a Fitzmorris and he'll never give in. He would rather die in rags. The Fitzmorris family has character. When he was a child, my great-great-great-grandfather, Lord Shatterton Fitzmorris, was rather put upon by the Duke of Wellester. The young duke placed a tack under my ancestor's seat, and everybody present on that occasion had a good laugh. My ancestor laughed too but at the same time was thinking, The first chance I get, I shall put a tack under Wellester's arse. Shortly thereafter, however, Wellester went off to France and my ancestor had to give up the idea. Wellester didn't return for twenty-five years. A revolution that had been brewing during that time finally blew up and the king was deposed. A plebiscite showed that Wellester was the people's choice for king, and a delegation of noblemen was sent to France to offer him the crown. He accepted. The history books tell how memorable his coronation was, particularly the moment when he took the throne. The new king, followed by two files of dignitaries, paraded down the nave, mounted the steps, and solemnly seated himself. He rose again suddenly and muttered an oath. Then a tall, dignified man stepped forward from the two ranks of dignitaries, approached the king, and knelt before him, saying, Your Majesty, for twenty-five years I have intrigued in the shadows, thrown half my fortune to the winds, risked my life, fought valiantly and finally I have been able to free our country from the tyranny of King Alfred. Today, then, is a day of satisfaction for all of us—for the people, because you are their chosen king, for you because you are our king, and for me, because finally I have been able to put a tack under your arse. —That man was of course Lord Shatterton Fitzmorris. Duncan is also a Fitzmorris. He therefore will never drink your foul castor oil. You knew it and you should never have put that clause in the will."

The late Mrs. Fitzmorris shook her head. "Your stories about your ancestors bore me. I'm only interested in my son's health. When I first asked him to drink the castor oil, he was six years old and hadn't had a good purge for seven months. At the time of my death he was thirty and needed it more than ever. A glass of castor oil is the bloom of health to any young body. I'm certain Duncan will drink it. He may have the Fitzmorris pigheadedness, but he must have some of the Mayberry brains to make up for it!"

These discussions on the cloud went on ad nauseam. For a while now Mr. Fitzmorris had been having a winning streak, but soon it had to be Mrs. Fitzmorris's turn. Mrs. Fitzmorris leaped for joy when she spotted Dickson and the two witnesses disembarking in the United States. "The Fitzmorrises are about to lose to the Mayberrys!" she cried gleefully. "Duncan's beginning to be worried. He'll drink it now!"

Every morning Mr. and Mrs. Fitzmorris would watch the scenes in the visitors' room. "He wouldn't drink it today!" Mr. Fitzmorris would crow triumphantly, inwardly sighing with relief. So the late Mrs. Fitzmorris had not yet had the satisfaction of saying to her husband, "What did I tell you, dear?"

This had gone on for quite a while. But one day something out of the ordinary happened. Mr. and Mrs. Fitzmorris were anxiously awaiting the arrival of Dickson and the two witnesses when they observed a strange scene. The lawyer and witnesses emerged from their carriage in front of the prison and walked off toward the entry. Suddenly two other carriages pulled up on either side of theirs and some men hopped out, laid hands on them, and hauled them into one of the carriages, all in a matter of seconds.

"That's illegal!" cried Mrs. Fitzmorris. "That's unfair! Just when Duncan was about to give in!"

Mr. Fitzmorris shrugged his shoulders. "I had nothing to do with it, Jasmine dear, I assure you."

Mr. Fitzmorris hadn't had the slightest responsibility for what had happened. Clotilda was behind it all, as usual. Clotilda was aware of Duncan's morning ritual with the lawyer and two witnesses. Septimius hadn't talked and Clegg didn't know about it. But Smithson one morning had overheard Dickson ask Duncan the usual question.

"The three of them show up every morning," a policeman told Smithson. "They go to the visitors' lounge and ask Fitzmorris to do something about some oil. He asks them to come again another day. They must be olive-oil salesmen or something."

Smithson related all this to Clotilda and her heart jumped. The inheritance! "If he asked his lawyer to come to America with the two witnesses, it means that rather than give in to me, he'll agree to that clause in his mother's will. He's got the perfect weapon at arm's length."

"Is it a large estate?"

"Two million pounds."

The lawyer spread his arms. "That's too much money for me—he'd be released in a couple of hours with personal apologies from the President."

So Clo decided to get rid of lawyer and witnesses and she had them kidnapped. Those three were now aboard the *Dolphin* cruising around the Caribbean. "In the long run, it's better than hanging around a prison for days on end," Dickson had commented. "Healthier, more amusing, and rather educative."

When he found out, Smithson was not very pleased with Clotilda. "Miss Troll," he said dryly, "we're in rather a tight spot as it is. The thing's gotten out of hand and you're making it a great deal worse by kidnapping three more men. Don't you realize that if this last is publicized, the situation will be very tragic indeed? Incidentally, why always *three?*" The lawyer shook his head. "I hope this turns out all right. Meanwhile, here are some more newspapers demanding your immediate arrest."

That night Clotilda received a visit from a police detective who very delicately asked her a lot of insignificant questions. It was the beginning of the end, and Clotilda couldn't sleep that night. The next day the American press pulled one of its usual exceptionally mean tricks: huge headlines about the Upstate Express Heist, complete with colored daguerreotypes, hypotheses, and protests. Overnight enormous posters appeared on every street corner with the following warning:

CITIZENS! Do not travel on the railways any more. They are the least secure method of transportation, as we have demonstrated to you by the recent theft of a passenger car from the middle of a train. If you would like to see this car, be at Pier 14 at 1 P.M. today. The thirty passengers, all safe and healthy, will vouch for the excellent treatment we gave them and, most importantly, for the demonstration of how unsafe it is to ride the railroads today. Citizens, do not use the railways, even for your long trips!

The citizens went down to Pier 14 and at 1 p.m. on the dot a ferry chugged in with the car from the Upstate Express. The thirty passengers debarked, very pleased with themselves. They'd all had a marvelous cruise, had been treated like pashas, and at the end had been paid quite a lot of money.

By whom? Evidently by the stagecoach and carriage companies. Who knows? And who knows how the car had been stolen? It was just as Duncan guessed.

(As I pointed out in the Digression, during this time I was a poor urchin and wasn't yet writing for the papers. I was working for my uncle Philip in Argentina. My uncle Philip was interested in the Argentine railways at the time, but occasionally he accepted commissions for work abroad. I am therefore in a position to vouch for the accuracy of Duncan Fitzmorris's hypothesis.

One flaw in it was that Duncan had not made a provision for reuniting the two halves of the train. Very simple: we built the spur just before the track went down a steep incline. As the locomotive section braked its speed, the rear section caught up and its momentum was sufficient to recouple the two sections.

The other flaw had to do with the man on the rear platform of the car, who, you will remember, was supposed to enter the car at a certain moment and point a pistol at the passengers to maintain order.

Not true. I didn't use one pistol, I used two. And another thing is, I wasn't yet a man. I was a poor urchin, just a poor innocent child.)

19

Mousquet narrates in his *Tales of the New World* that a certain Fred Merton of San Francisco got drunk on gin and passed out two hours before the earthquake that caused the great fire that destroyed the city. Twenty-four hours later, Fred Merton woke up. The only thing standing in all San Francisco was the wing of his mansion in which he'd passed out. "Well, well," said Mr. Merton, trying to light the gas lamp in his room, "the valve must be broken."

Thus it was that Duncan, on the afternoon of the events of the preceding chapter, upon the entrance into his cell of a frowning official, stopped musing on the story of Fred Merton, though not entirely. "Well, well," he reflected, "the thing's got more mucked up." Then he apathetically followed the official out of his cell and soon found himself before a group of very solemn gentlemen.

"Mr. Fitzmorris," the most dignified-looking of them said, "as you know, the case of the Upstate Express Robbery has been solved . . ."

"I beg Your Honor's pardon," Duncan put in politely, "but I haven't been able to keep abreast of events from my present accommodations. I don't know anything at all about this Express Upstate or whatever you call it."

"Wonderful," His Honor sighed, "you're probably

the only person in the U.S. who doesn't. At any rate, the important thing is that what's happened has made a shambles of the case against you. Allow us to convey our profound apologies for connecting you with that disgraceful incident. We simply didn't see things clearly. In fact, we still don't understand why, being the law-abiding citizen which according to all indications you are, you did not expose the real smugglers aboard the *Jeannette*."

Duncan couldn't say, "For love of Kitty"; a law-abiding citizen should never protect a smuggler even if she does happen to be a gorgeous blonde.

"They wouldn't let us say anything," Duncan answered. "In any case I wasn't the only one, the other two didn't speak up either . . ."

"The other two don't count," His Honor interrupted ferociously. "The other two are just run-of-the-mill half-wits. Now let's have it. We have positive evidence that you were on the *Oasis in the Ocean* with your two friends and Miss Troll. Now why did you make up the story about the shipwreck and persuade Miss Troll to say she'd never set eyes on you before when in fact she posted your bail the first time you were arrested?"

Duncan couldn't open his mouth. How could he admit he had been the unconscious accomplice of the pirates? "It's a rather delicate subject," Duncan said. "The reputation of a lady who had been alone with me for several days on an island . . . you understand, Your Honor . . . people are malicious . . ."

His Honor shook his head. "I have the impression that you, Mr. Fitzmorris, were bored with your two million pounds and came over here for the express purpose of making hash of the American police. In any case we shall have to investigate this more carefully. There are too many loose ends. We'll free you, but only on restricted parole. You and your friends will have to check in with Commissioner Brenner every five hours. Except at night. Then we'll be watching your every dream."

"We're worse off than before," Duncan observed when he found himself on the street with Clegg and Septimius. "We haven't a penny, and since we must check in every five hours, what job could we take? When you consider the amount of time it takes to get here and back, this so-called parole is just a walking prison. I'll have to ask Dickson for a loan. I haven't seen him in two days."

Clegg had a couple of dollars and politely offered them to Duncan. Then Duncan suddenly remembered what Septimius had told him.

"As for you, I thought you were a gentleman," Duncan said accusingly. "Instead it appears you're nothing but a spy. You ought to be ashamed of yourself."

Poor Clegg began to cry. "I'm very sorry, Mr. Fitzmorris. I didn't do it out of malice. Miss Troll wanted me to."

"How much is she paying you?" asked Duncan.

"Well . . . she promised me a kiss a month. No, now it's two, since she doubled my salary the other day."

Duncan was appalled. "You're totally brainless, Clegg. To sell yourself for a woman's kisses is worse than to do it for money."

Septimius interrupted. "Let's go into that coffee shop," he said. "I've got a plan."

The three men went in and took a corner booth.

"Clegg, hand over your two dollars," Septimius said. Clegg pushed the two bills across the table.

"Now let's have the leg." Septimius laid his huge hand on Clegg's shoulder.

Clegg obeyed without a word. He fiddled around under the table for a moment and then put his leg into

Septimius's hands. Septimius wrapped it up in a news-paper and called the waiter to pay the bill.

"Bring this man a coffee every two hours. I'll pay you when I come back."

As they left he said to Duncan, "That takes care of him."

Clegg's dollar bill took them as far as the hotel Dickson and the witnesses were staying at; the desk clerk told them they had checked out. Two sailors had come to pay the bill and collect their baggage.

"Sailors?" Duncan was astonished. "What kind of sailors?"

"Foreigners," the clerk said. "Queerest English I ever heard. Some fool name written on their caps."

"*Dolphin?*" Duncan asked anxiously.

"That's it, *Dolphin*."

The two men went off very depressed. "That idiot girl has fouled us up again!" Duncan exclaimed angrily after a long silence. "Who knows where she sent Dickson!"

Septimius made a suggestion. "Let's go see if the agency can help."

It was an intelligent proposal.

At the sight of the two men, Peggy burst into tears. The fat man gave Duncan all the money he had stashed away in his numerous pockets.

"You'd better keep in touch with us," Peggy said after Duncan explained the situation.

The two men caught a streetcar. The five hours were almost up and it was time to put Clegg back together. At the police station they were forced to sign a register and account for all their movements during the five hours.

"We went for a walk," Duncan said indifferently.

"Sure," the sergeant said. "First you walked to the

Swank Coffee Shoppe, one of you stayed behind there, then you walked to the Roundtree Hotel on Astor Place, then to the Acme Agency on Twelfth Street. Tonight you're walking to the Newberry Hotel, where I've reserved a room for you. Grills on the window. So the mosquitoes can't come in."

Duncan was gloomy when they came out of the police station. The three men walked on in silence. They were being followed.

They spotted their shadows immediately: two ugly brutes. Even a child could have picked them out. One did: "Look, Mama, two gumshoes!"

This made everything twice as bad: they had to keep going to the agency to keep up with new developments but this would arouse the detectives' suspicions—and no doubt they would try to foil any plans. Duncan quickly proposed a solution. "Septimius," he said when they'd reached their hotel, "take a carriage uptown to Central Park. Stay there for an hour and then come back here."

Septimius went off and one of the shadows followed him.

"Now, Mr. Clegg, you take a streetcar downtown. Come back in an hour."

Clegg, glad to be of some use, hopped on a streetcar to Wall Street, which left the other shadow a bit confused. Duncan helped him make up his mind by going inside the hotel. The shadow jumped on the next streetcar and made off after Clegg.

Five minutes later Duncan was at the agency. He explained the delay. "This whole thing is too much," he concluded. But the fat man was laughing. "Give Chico a ring," he told Peggy. "As for you, Mr. Fitzmorris, don't leave your hotel. Just buy every edition of the *Sun*."

A boy with curls on his forehead came in.

(At this point I wasn't writing for the newspapers yet. I was just a poor boy, God's creature being tossed around by fate, far away from his twenty-two brothers and sisters. I was working for my uncle Philip, but fate wasn't working for me and I had been the victim of chance. Chance had it, unfortunately, that the forehead of some man in uniform had gotten in the way of a bullet from my gun and I had to leave Mexico and come to New York City.

Anyhow, I was a poor boy. What could I do for a living? Be a newsboy. So I hawked the *Sun*.)

"Remember this gentleman's face," the fat man said, pointing to Mr. Fitzmorris. "You'll be selling him the *Sun*."

Duncan went back to the hotel and soon Septimius and Clegg showed up, followed by their shadows. A couple of hours later they heard the second afternoon edition being hawked in the street. Duncan went outside and approached the *Sun* newsboy. He bought a copy of the *Sun*, opened it, and found a note pinned to page 3 that said: "Nothing new."

The two evening editions didn't have anything more interesting to report and the night went by slowly and sadly. The first morning edition didn't promise anything either. But the midday edition had sensational news. *Tonight at eight on the dot be at the Union Square taxi stand. Get in #471, come out the other side and get into the next cab, #525. He'll take you to a motor launch. That will take you to the* Grilling, *which sails at 8:30. Remember me. Love, Peggy.*

"Perfect," said Duncan, tearing the note to tiny pieces. But that wasn't all the sensational news. During luncheon at the hotel the waiter while serving some chocolate cake whispered to Duncan that a blond woman would meet him at seven o'clock at the restaurant across the street from Mrs. Thompson's house.

"That has to be Kitty," Duncan thought. "We'd better be careful about Clegg."

After they checked in with the police, Duncan told Septimius to dismember Clegg. Septimius threw Clegg on the bed, wrapped his leg up in newspapers, and tucked it under his arm. Outside the hotel, Duncan explained everything to Septimius. They would come back to get Clegg after the meeting with Kitty. So, to prevent Clegg from tipping off Clotilda, they would divide the opposition: one of the shadows had to stay behind at the hotel to guard Clegg. They slowly made their way over to Mrs. Thompson's, went into the restaurant across the street, took the only free table, and ordered coffee. The band and the people around them made a lot of noise. A cigarette girl came by their table. She was a handsome brunette who didn't look a bit like Kitty. Of course she was Kitty.

"Everything's going fine. I'm sailing tonight on the *Grilling*," he said, taking the pack of cigarettes she offered him.

"They're the best, sir," Kitty said, smiling. "Each one contains a fifty-dollar bill. Good luck, darling." All in a normal tone of voice.

"Marvelous, that girl," Duncan said admiringly to Septimius when they were out on the street. "God only knows what she had to go through to get some policeman to tell her what hotel we were staying at."

Septimius was deeply moved. "If I ever found a girl who loved me like that," he exclaimed, "I'd be the strongest man in the world!"

Duncan smiled. "You might feel like the strongest," he said, "but actually you would be the weakest."

"Right," Septimius said, though he hadn't grasped

Duncan's meaning. "Maybe that's better, anyway."

In 1905 New York City was not quite the same as it is today. It was a circus already, to be sure, but only a two-ring circus. One could never find carriages or street-cars when one needed them, and one wasted a good deal of time trying to find them. Duncan and Septimius weren't having much luck as far as transportation went. At seven-forty they were only halfway back to the hotel. There was barely time to get to Union Square on time. When they arrived, it was precisely eight.

Standing in front of cab #471, Duncan pulled out his watch and said very loud for the shadow's benefit, "Oh my! It's eight o'clock. We must run back to the hotel! Here, let's take this cab."

Number 471 was a closed carriage. Duncan and Septimius got in quickly and slammed the door. "Hurry, shout the address to the driver and get out fast!" said somebody already inside #471.

"Hotel Newberry!" Duncan shouted, sticking his head out the window. Then he joined Septimius in #525.

The two men safely inside #525 watched #471 careen down the street, the shadow's cab faithfully tailing it.

A sigh of relief. Then, after a rocky gallop, they saw the sea sparkling. They jumped out of the cab and dropped onto the deck of a big motor launch. A fast trip across the water and there, finally, was the profile of the *Grilling* against the last rays of the sun. It was gliding along gently and by the time Duncan and Septimius got aboard they were already outside New York Harbor.

"If our luck doesn't turn sour in the next half hour," Duncan exclaimed, "we shall never have to hear about this infernal city or that idiotic girl again!"

A sailor approached them. "Miss Troll expects you in the stern parlor," he said.

20

Duncan stiffened. "What did you say?" he said tensely as Septimius covered his eyes.

"Miss Troll expects you in the stern parlor," the sailor repeated. "Dinner is served."

Septimius proposed a solution. "We could swim to shore, I'm sure of it."

"I'm sure of it too," Duncan answered. "But I've no intention of being picked up by the harbor police again. Let's go have dinner."

"Maybe that's better," Septimius agreed. "This evening air makes one ravenous."

The two men followed the sailor. A door opened and the light from inside poured out onto the darkened deck. The small table in the middle of the room was a triumph of lace, crystal, and flowers. Clotilda appeared between two bouquets of roses, one red and one yellow. Evidently this was supposed to create a special effect.

"Good evening, Mr. Fitzmorris, Mr. North," Clotilda said, smiling amiably. "Come in, come in, Mr. Clegg."

Septimius turned to Duncan. In their flight they'd forgotten Clegg. Septimius felt the weight of Clegg's leg on his arm and turned white. Even Duncan frowned and wouldn't look Clotilda in the eye.

"Where is Clegg?" Clotilda asked, alarmed.

Duncan lowered his head. Septimius gazed at the ceiling.

"What have you done with Clegg? What's happened to him? For heaven's sake, somebody say something!"

At this point Septimius, with the best intentions in the world, did something extremely stupid. He slowly unwrapped the newspapers and showed Clotilda Clegg's leg. "There you are," Septimius said.

Clotilda didn't give him a chance to explain. She let out a shriek and flew to a corner of the room in terror. "That's hideous!" she sobbed. Then she pointed an accusing finger at both men. "You killed him when you found out he worked for me!"

Duncan smiled. "Miss Troll is exaggerating when she says we did away with Clegg, isn't she, Septimius?"

"I should think so, Duncan," Septimius answered, tapping Clegg's leg with his knuckles. "This is only a wooden leg. The rest of him, flesh and blood, is at the Hotel Newberry. We forgot to bring him along."

Clotilda felt ridiculous. "I didn't know he had a wooden leg," she said. "At any rate it's dreadful of you to take a man's support away from him and prevent him from saving himself."

Duncan shook his head. "It really did happen quite by accident," he explained. "We didn't suspect this escape on the *Grilling* was one of your interesting little machinations, and since we knew Clegg was in your pay at the rate of one—no, two kisses a month, we decided to immobilize Clegg until we were about to leave. But we didn't calculate the time right and Clegg got left at the hotel. However," Duncan added, "I assure you I'd willingly change places with him. It's certainly a great deal safer to be in the clutches of the American police than in those of Clotilda Troll."

Clotilda had collected herself. "Anybody who expects

gratitude from a human being is a fool," she sighed. "But I'm no fool and I certainly harbored no hopes. If I got you out of the mess you were in, I did it merely for compassion's sake."

Clotilda took her seat and motioned for them to sit down. Exquisite food, wine, and fruit were served, but they avoided talking. After she'd finished her coffee, Clotilda turned to Septimius with a smile. "Mr. North, I'm sure you'd like to retire now. You must be emotionally and physically exhausted. Don't worry about us. Your cabin is all made up."

Septimius caught her gist. He thanked her, said good night, and started to go out. Then he remembered having left something behind and went to pick up Clegg's leg in the corner.

"Septimius," Duncan said then, "would you be good enough to ask Miss Troll if she would pay Mr. Clegg's wages in absentia to his leg. After all, it's the end of the month and it deserves a kiss, poor put-upon leg."

Septimius was a dear boy. "Ha, ha!" he snickered. As he went out he kept slapping Clegg's thigh with mirth. They could hear him laughing for quite a while.

When everything was quiet again, Clotilda picked a flower from one of the vases and sniffed it gracefully. Apparently she was about to speak. But Duncan didn't give her time. "Miss Troll," he said firmly, "I think this practical joke has passed the boundaries of good taste and discretion. To go on like this would be grotesque. I would not want to call this last installment piracy. I know it solved a sticky problem for you. I therefore would like to be reasonable about it. I'm sure the Upstate Express business had nothing to do with you . . ."

"You're quite wrong there, Mr. Fitzmorris," Clotilda interrupted him. "Actually it's entirely owing to me if for a few days you were the most famous man in America. I put Smithson up to it."

It took Duncan a moment to recover. He hadn't expected that.

"All right, we'll throw that in with the rest and be done with it. Enough is quite enough, Miss Troll. Now will you please come back to the world of the sane and tell the captain to set our course for New Islip. After you drop us off there you can come back for Clegg and Smithson and go wherever you like. To the devil, I hope!"

"I can't tell you what pleasure it gives me to hear a Fitzmorris use language like that," Clotilda exclaimed gleefully. "I also have the pleasure of informing you that I shall most certainly *not* steer for New Islip. We're only a sloop and it would be folly to attempt that long crossing. Before I go through with my plan I have two suggestions. One, that you humbly beg my pardon for all the insults you've heaped on me, and two, that you even more humbly ask me to marry you."

"I'd rather drink ten gallons of castor oil than marry you!" Duncan shouted.

"I appreciate your healthful inclinations," Clotilda acknowledged, "but it will be a bit of a chore for you to find the lawyer who's carting around that famous glass of castor oil. At the moment he's cruising around seeing wonderful sights from the deck of the *Dolphin*. The ocean's quite a big place. Who knows if he'll ever be found again. We are on our way to Argentina now, Mr. Fitzmorris. I guarantee you'll have a bad time of it in Argentina. I've a great many friends in Argentina and they shall help me. You ought to give in, Mr. Fitzmorris. I shall have such fun the day you ask me to marry you."

Duncan slowly rose from his chair and approached

Clotilda. Ranks of Fitzmorris ancestors from A.D. 1000 to 1700, clouds of knights and impeccable gentlemen were shouting their indignation at him from the past. But Duncan wasn't listening. Duncan was going to take Clotilda by her beautiful tresses, put her over his knee, and give her a horrendous spanking.

Clotilda realized nobody could stop his ferocious advance and she didn't bother to ring for help. She retreated to a corner and awaited the worst, her eyes squeezed shut. She waited with avid delight. Then a sudden clamor interrupted Duncan's advance. The *Grilling* lurched violently and angry shouts broke out on deck. The door flew open, and there stood Kitty, revolver in hand.

It wasn't mere chance that brought the gorgeous smuggler to the decks of the *Grilling*, nor had she fallen out of the sky. The *Grilling* had raised anchor from New York harbor at 8:30, and at nine o'clock that same night Georgie and Kitty (once again a blonde after her job at the restaurant) were chatting gaily in the lobby of the Brevoort.

"I'm very happy," said Georgie at one point. "That idiotic girl seems to have cleared out finally. Evidently all this publicity and the trouble the police gave her convinced her to slip away unnoticed. I rented a good sloop for her and she's leaving tonight for Argentina. In fact, she left half an hour ago."

Kitty grabbed Georgie's sleeve. "What's the name of that sloop?" she asked, a horrible thought crossing her mind.

"The *Grilling*," Georgie said.

After that, Georgie didn't know what was happening. He had no choice but to let Kitty drag him around by the arm. They found a carriage and galloped through the streets, then a train, then another carriage; he had no idea where they were headed in the dark of the night.

Finally he saw the sea shimmering under the moon. He wanted to question her, but Kitty was already banging on a door. When the door opened, twenty voices said with delighted surprise, "The boss!"

So Georgie, impeccable New Islip gentleman, found himself in the smugglers' lair in Saxton.

Kitty took Bill to one side. "Are the boilers hot on the *Jeannette?*"

"Sure, Kitty. We were just about to take off for . . ."

"Never mind that!" Kitty ordered. "Get the men aboard, stoke up a good head of steam. We've got to catch up with a sloop called the *Grilling*."

"Where is this sloop?" Bill asked, astounded.

"At sea! Where else, you idiot?" Kitty cried. "She set sail at 8:30 from New York and she's headed for Argentina. It's eleven now. In two and a half hours they can't have gotten very far. They must be following the coastline. If we get a move on, we can cut them off."

Georgie in this kind of situation as a rule made himself comfortable in an armchair and kept his mouth shut. Since there weren't any free chairs in the room, he kept quiet standing up. He didn't leave Kitty's side and went aboard the *Jeannette* without a word. When they were on deck, Kitty suddenly pushed a revolver at him. Caught off guard, Georgie went white and put up his hands, stammering, "But, Kitty, I love you . . ."

"That's why!" Kitty said. "Put down your hands and take this. We're going to need them."

"What is going on?" Georgie was still stuttering.

Kitty was acting like Captain Blood to the rescue. Georgie sat down on a coil of hemp and held his head between his hands.

But it turned out there was no need of guns. Aside from the helmsman, most of the *Grilling's* crew were sound asleep when the *Jeannette* intercepted her. A quick lashing and two seconds later Kitty, followed by Georgie and fifteen smugglers, was on the *Grilling's* deck, mistress of the situation. She flew to the door of the stern parlor and threw it open.

"Good evening, Miss Troll," said Kitty sarcastically, toying with her revolver. "You may be a splendid millionairess, but I'm definitely the better pirate. Even Morgan never carried off a boarding this well."

Terrified, Clotilda counted the fifteen huge men. This time she was really afraid.

"Bill," Kitty commanded, "take care of the crew. Be gentle about it, I don't want any massacres."

"Right," Bill said, going out with his men. "We'll play some puss-in-the-corner to keep ourselves amused."

"Don't make such a point of being stupid, will you?" Kitty exclaimed without turning around. "Keep the two ships about twenty yards apart. We're too near the coast and we don't need any surprises."

Georgie came in unobtrusively. There was, happily, an armchair in the parlor, and Georgie sat down and as usual kept his mouth shut, but this time in more comfort. Duncan, at first overcome by surprise, turned to Kitty.

"Kitty," he said admiringly, "you're an extraordinary woman, and if I were ever to envy anyone, it would be Georgie, who's had the good sense to capture your heart. You shouldn't let people call you a countess. It's an insult to your honor as a smuggler."

Kitty blushed with pride.

"I thank you, my blond pirate friend," Duncan concluded, bowing. Georgie felt very moved and very proud. It was rather nice being the fiancé of Captain Blood-to-the-rescue.

Clotilda meanwhile had pulled herself together and was preparing to deliver one of her usual song-and-dances. "What a very pleasant surprise, Countess," she began.

But Kitty wasn't about to let her continue. "This is no time for chit-chat, Miss Troll. I'm running this show now and I'll do the talking. The game is over. You're going back to New York and Duncan is going wherever he wants to. So sit down and shut up."

Kitty brandished her revolver wildly as she talked. Clotilda turned gray, sat down in the corner, and began to sob.

"Now then," Kitty said, turning to Duncan. "What do you want me to do?"

"Well, for one thing, how about putting away that gun you've been waving around as if it were a flower or something," Duncan said. Kitty smiled and put the revolver in her pocket.

Duncan thought quietly for a moment, then beamed at Kitty. Evidently he'd found the solution. At that point the door banged open and in stormed Septimius in his dressing gown. "Duncan, the pirates!" he cried in alarm.

"Very good, Septimius," Duncan approved. "That's quite right. Now sit down over there and listen."

Septimius looked at Kitty respectfully. "Don't tell me we're starting all over again?" he asked.

"No," Duncan reassured him. "This time we're ending it." Then he revealed his plan. "It's about time Septimius and I went back to New Islip. We'll send Clegg's leg to our consulate in New York and when the consul returns to America he'll straighten everything out. It's impossible to sail the *Grilling* to New Islip, and besides, we must track down Dickson and my witnesses, who are on the *Dolphin*. Therefore I propose we begin looking for the *Dolphin,* which must be somewhere in the vicinity. Then Septimius and I will take the *Dolphin* back to New Islip. Kitty and Georgie, you'll escort Miss Troll back to New York."

Kitty shook her head. "What am I going to do about my twenty men?"

"They . . . they could go back alone," Georgie suggested. "I'd be willing to pay them for their trouble. Anyway, Kitty, what would you and I do in New York? Why don't you come back to New Islip with me?"

Kitty looked at Georgie and then at Duncan. Duncan nodded approval. "Very sensible proposal, Georgie," he exclaimed. "We'll change the plan. Send all the men back immediately. Then, once we find her, we'll change over to the *Dolphin* and Miss Troll can go wherever she wants on the *Grilling.*"

Kitty was confused and her eyes flew back and forth between Duncan and Georgie.

"It will be a new life," Duncan said to her. "A life of tranquillity and honesty."

"Yes, yes," said Kitty, very moved.

"Will a hundred dollars a head take care of your men?" asked Georgie, who couldn't wait to see the last of the smugglers.

"Don't be silly," she answered. "Fifty will do it. Let's not start throwing our money around."

With trembling hands, Georgie pulled out twenty fifty-dollar bills and handed them to Kitty. Kitty went out and called Bill. "Bill, you have to go back right away. The plan blew up in my face. Here's five hundred dollars for you. Make sure the men are happy. I'm staying here."

Bill couldn't argue with five hundred dollars. He called the men together. "Look here, men, the job fell through and we've got to take a powder. Kitty didn't forget you, though. Here's fifty dollars out of her own pocket to tide you over. Split it up and make sure the five guys back on the boat get a piece of it."

The *Jeannette* pulled up alongside and Bill followed the fifteen men on board.

"How'd it go?" the five men who had stayed on board asked.

"Didn't pan out," the others answered. "They didn't even have enough small change to tide us over."

The *Jeanette* steamed off at full speed. Georgie sighed with relief and Clotilda felt stronger, quite a lot stronger. "A bit of quiet after all this commotion would do us all good," she said, stifling a yawn behind her handkerchief. "I'm sorry to desert such pleasant company, but I must go to bed."

"Miss Troll, no more pranks," Duncan said. "Where is the *Dolphin?*"

"Oh, that's such a long story," Clotilda sighed, going out. "Very, very complicated." Evidently there was nothing they could do.

Before Clotilda left, Kitty politely stopped her. "I'm so sorry, Miss Troll," she apologized, "but I'll have to spend the night with you. The thought of spending it alone in a cabin among all these men terrifies me."

"I'm sorry too, because my maid sleeps in the other berth in my cabin."

"That's perfectly all right, Miss Troll. I don't mind sleeping in the same bed with you."

Clotilda saw it was unwise to continue disagreeing and went out, followed by Kitty. Duncan, Septimius, and Georgie looked at each other.

"This *is* a mess," Septimius noted.

"Maybe it's a better idea to persuade her gently," Georgie said after a quarter of an hour.

Duncan didn't answer. He just smiled knowingly.

Shortly thereafter Kitty reappeared, gracefully wrapped in one of Clotilda's dressing gowns. "Miss Troll," Kitty explained, "tells me that the *Dolphin*'s meeting us tomorrow when our pilot steers for Nassau. Good night, gentlemen. Sleep well, Georgie dear."

"Did you see that?" Georgie exclaimed, very pleased. "She's not a bad sort, that Clotilda. You have to know how to handle her."

Meanwhile Clotilda, lying face down on her berth—it was the only comfortable position after Kitty's persuasive arguments—was hurling abuse at Kitty, in the other berth. "I will have you hanged when we get to New Islip!"

"We'll talk about it when we get there, Miss Troll. If when you were a child somebody had given you the sort of lesson you got tonight, you wouldn't be in the unpleasant position you're in now."

"I will not sleep with one leg tied to the bedpost!" Clotilda said through clenched teeth.

"So don't sleep," Kitty said, turning out the light.

At ten o'clock the *Grilling* met the *Dolphin*.

"Now we shall see who's in charge," Clotilda said to Kitty in her cabin. "We'll just see which one of us the captain of the *Dolphin* obeys."

Kitty got out of bed and shook her head sadly. "It's a shame for a kindhearted woman like me to have to gag a nice girl like you," Kitty sighed as she picked up a large towel.

Clotilda backed off in terror. Kitty grabbed her by the hair and laid her out flat on the bed. Clo didn't put up a fight. She gave up and began to sob.

"Kitty, give me another spanking if you want, but please take me aboard the *Dolphin* with you. I did all this only because I'm in love with Duncan. Come on, Kitty . . ."

Kitty let go of Clotilda's hair and tossed the towel away. "Miss Troll," she said in the fiercest voice she could muster, "I'll let you come aboard the *Dolphin,* but if you try to pull anything, I assure you I'll have you thrown overboard."

Clotilda raised her tear-streaked face and looked at Kitty. "Thank you, Kitty," she said. The blond smuggler turned away to hide her blush. Idiotic girl! But Kitty knew from experience that she was going to have to keep a close eye on Clotilda.

The *Grilling* was sent back to New York. The captain and crew were generously paid off. The *Dolphin's* captain asked Miss Troll what her destination was to be and Kitty watched her face. But Clo didn't hesitate. "New Islip, full steam ahead!"

Dickson and the two witnesses greeted Duncan unenthusiastically. "Are you planning on going to jail when you get home?" the lawyer said after a long silence.

"I don't know," Duncan said, laughing. "Depends on the circumstances."

So there they were again on the *Dolphin* just as they had been at the beginning, minus Clegg, of course, wholly absent now that they had sent his leg stuffed with money and their best wishes back to New York. Plus Dickson, two witnesses, Clotilda, Kitty, and Georgie.

Kitty had left off keeping an eye on Clotilda and was concentrating entirely on Georgie. Once in a while she glanced at the sea, and as America's coastline became more and more distant, she felt less and less like a smuggler. Georgie sat in an armchair next to her with his mouth shut, but this time he was happy about it.

Septimius, locked up with the captain in his cabin, was rolling dice, winning (naturally), shooting one pair of boxcars after another.

The lawyer and two witnesses ate and slept.

Clotilda would not come out of her cabin. She was depressed. She had visions of New Islip, the quiet streets, the usual friends. Once in a while she ran into Duncan in these fantasies and Duncan greeted her with the same apathy as before. Everything was back to normal and Duncan's fate no longer went by the name of Clotilda.

What about Duncan? Well, Duncan was depressed too. In fact, Duncan might have been the saddest man on earth, the victim of his own backbone of steel.

Duncan too envisioned New Islip, its quiet streets, the usual social circle. A vision that reeked of castor oil.

The adventure was over. Clotilda was again Miss Troll, rich, foolish heiress who went for strolls, to the races, to charity balls. Her insane project had come to a miserable close. Poor idiotic girl. Duncan felt a bit sorry for her. Because if Clotilda was seriously in love with him, it made everything very melancholy indeed.

"Let's hope she really isn't in love with me," Duncan thought.

So the yacht glided along under the sun and moon and they all ate without speaking to each other. Clotilda avoided everybody's eyes, like a child who's been found out.

Then one day towards sunset the captain announced: "We've sighted New Islip harbor."

21

Georgie and Kitty were the last to debark. The captain, before he would let the couple off, squeezed a hundred dollars out of her to cover the cost of repairing a few irregularities in her passport.

The lawyer and witnesses got off immediately. "You know where to find us, Mr. Fitzmorris," Dickson said before he left the ship. Duncan nodded his head solemnly.

Then Septimius started down the gangplank, after embracing Duncan with tears in his eyes.

Then Duncan debarked and Clotilda followed behind him. "Good night, Miss Troll."

"Good night, Mr. Fitzmorris." Clotilda's voice was strained; she was expecting some sarcastic remark from Duncan. But Duncan was a man of good taste.

Duncan had some money—four hundred dollars Kitty had passed him in the cigarettes from the restaurant opposite Mrs. Thompson's. He went off to a hotel.

How long would that pittance last? And then what?

Then he was going to have to drink that foul castor oil. The whole thing was ridiculous. Duncan was quite annoyed with his mother and her impossible codicil. It had been thoroughly inconsiderate of her. He would never stoop to drink it.

The New Islip air revived all of Duncan's Fitzmorris bullheadedness.

"And that little idiot," Duncan asked himself, "what on earth made her cook up a wild scheme like that? What could she hope to gain?"

Two, three, four intolerably dreary days went by. The fifth night Duncan found himself walking in front of the Trolls' imposing town house. "I'd rather like it if Clotilda came out right now," Duncan said to himself. "I wonder if she's up to her old tricks."

But Clotilda didn't come out. Clotilda was locked in her room crying on Kitty's shoulder. Kitty was shaking her head and muttering, "You poor thing! I ask myself, has any man ever been so hardhearted?"

It was an evening in August, or perhaps September— anyhow, it was a beautiful evening, that was the important thing—and the municipal park of New Islip was quiet and deserted. The branches of the trees were scattering the last red rays of the setting sun when Duncan unexpectedly ran into Clotilda. Neither of them had planned it. Clotilda was supposed to be meeting Kitty, and so was Duncan.

Duncan only had three shillings in his pocket and he thought he saw an ambiguous smile on Clotilda's face. Clotilda's heart was filled with bitterness and she thought she saw an ambiguous smile on Duncan's face. They therefore greeted each other with a certain amount of hostility, one might almost say with hatred.

"Good evening, Miss Troll."

"Good evening, Mr. Fitzmorris."

"Evidently there's been some mix-up. I wasn't expecting you," he explained.

"I wasn't expecting you either," Clotilda said with pride.

Duncan bowed perfunctorily, turned on his heel, and went off with his nose in the air.

At that moment, up on the family cloud, Mr. Fitzmorris said indignantly to his wife: "My dear, your son is a cretin."

"I agree completely. A total cretin," she said, laughing, and added, "Now let's go, Tom."

The cloud headed off toward the setting sun as the late Mr. Fitzmorris laughed until the tears came. "What a hopeless clown he is, my dear!"

Duncan had in fact strutted about twenty steps off, executed another about-face, walked firmly back toward Clotilda, who was still standing there with her mouth wide open, drew her to him, and kissed her like any ordinary cretin in love.

EPILOGUE

When Duncan married Clotilda, everybody was there: Mr. Georgie Ludens and his wife, Kitty, Mr. Septimius North, and Mr. Barton Clegg, just returned from America. Even Mr. and Mrs. Fitzmorris were there in spirit, on the family cloud.

Mr. Fitzmorris was beaming. "You see, my dear, the Fitzmorrises won after all. If I'm not mistaken, that's Clotilda Troll Duncan's marrying, and she's filthy rich. Now he can comfortably thumb his nose at your money and your glass of castor oil."

The late Mrs. Fitzmorris refused to answer her husband. After all, wasn't it better, thanks to her castor oil, that Duncan had turned down two million pounds and in compensation found happiness?

They spent their honeymoon on the *Dolphin* and it was magnificent.

"I've always loved you," Clotilda would say every now and then.

"I'd always loved you too," Duncan would answer, "but I didn't know it. I understood late, but not too late."

Then, after a long cruise, Duncan and Clo returned to New Islip to their handsome new house, a present from Mr. Troll.

AFTERWORD

One morning Duncan was quietly lying in bed when Clotilda came in, delicious in her flowered nightgown. It was a beautiful spring day. Clotilda was carrying a tray with a glass on it. "Duncan dear, drink this, it'll do you good," Clotilda said, smiling.

Duncan looked with alarm at the glass. "What is it?"

"Castor oil. Best thing for the springtime. You need it, Duncan."

Duncan shook his head. "I will never drink that filthy ooze," he declared violently.

Clotilda blushed and her eyes filled with tears. "Forgive me, Duncan," she whispered humbly. "I thought it might do you good. I'm sorry if I offended you."

That sweet face drenched in tears made Duncan feel like the most abject man on earth.

"Clotilda," he exclaimed, "hand over that glass." Clotilda held out the tray, terrified. "Clo, you know how much I hate this foul liquid. I wouldn't take it from my mother, and goodness knows how much that cost me, this hateful castor oil. Well . . ." He closed his eyes, held his nose, put the glass to his lips, and drank it all down in one gulp. ". . . I won't refuse yours!"

Clotilda gave a little squeal of delight and from behind a curtain emerged Dickson and the two witnesses.

"The castor oil has been drunk," the lawyer announced. "The estate is at your disposal from this moment on."

Duncan scowled at Clotilda, but Clo just caressed him sweetly. "You don't know how depressing it's been for me every day to think you only married me so you wouldn't have to drink that castor oil . . ."

Duncan shrugged. "I suppose it wasn't that bad, and maybe it will even do me some good. Perhaps my mother was right."

APPENDIX

Clotilda gave Duncan a peck on the cheek and ran off to her study, where someone was waiting for her.

"Mama, mama, I did it!" cried Clotilda, glowing with pride. "Thank heavens. Now we can cover the dairy farm's deficit, pay for this house Daddy gave us, have the *Dolphin* spruced up, and I need a whole new wardrobe. What traveling does to clothes!"

"Don't forget the mortgage on *our* house," said Mrs. Troll. "And then there was that ridiculous trip of yours. Lucky for you it worked. Here, I've totaled it all up roughly. You'd best write me out a check for a million pounds right now. That should leave the two of you enough to live on, for a while at least."

"The best thing about it is that finally I'm really in love," said Clotilda, all choked up. She threw open the window and gulped in the spring air.